D r. Dragonbreath pointed to Rule Number Five without saying a word. Almost all of the students followed his claw and instinctively read the rule to themselves. Here is what it said:

RULE NUMBER FIVE. THIS IS THE FORBIDDEN RULE. NO STUDENT IS ALLOWED TO READ THIS SENTENCE.

With his keen dragon eyes enhanced all the more by his magical dragon glasses, Dr. Dragonbreath took mental note of every single student who was reading Rule Number Five and therefore breaking Rule Number Five.

After reading the rule, all the students looked up at Dr. Dragonbreath nervously. He took off his glasses, loosened his tie, and smiled for the first time.

"Oh, you poor things. I had such high hopes for you."

Also by Derek the Ghost:

Scary School #2: Monsters on the March

SCARY SCHOOL

By

DEREK THE GHOST

Scary pictures by

SCOTT M. FISCHER

HARPER
An Imprint of HarperCollinsPublishers

Library of Congress Cataloging-in-Publication Data
Kent, Derek Taylor.
  Scary School / by Derek the Ghost ; scary pictures by Scott M.
Fischer. — 1st ed.
    p. cm.
  Summary: Describes a year at Scary School, where werewolves,
zombies, and humans mingle and the teachers range from dragons
to vampires.
  ISBN 978-0-06-196094-9
  [1. Supernatural—Fiction. 2. Schools—Fiction. 3. Humorous
stories.] I. Fischer, Scott M., ill. ll. Title.
PZ7.K4132Sc 2011   2010015223
[Fic]—dc22   CIP
                                                            AC

Typography by Erin Fitzsimmons
13 14 15 16   LP/BR   10 9 8 7 6 5 4 3 2
❖
First paperback edition, 2012

To Eric Myers, Dr. Levy,
Mr. Cooper-Mead,
Ms. O'Callaghan, Ms. Russell,
and all teachers who are
more inspiring than scary.

Contents

Caveat
discipulus

Introduction

I suppose the proper way to start an introduction is *with* an introduction, so . . . Hello! My name is Derek the Ghost. What's yours? I know you probably didn't say your name out loud just now, but I read your mind, and I want you to know that I think you have a fantastic name.

How did I read your mind? Let me tell you.

Last year, when I was just eleven years old, I died in science class. One of Mr. Acidbath's experiments went terribly wrong (more about that later), but things like that happen all the time at Scary School, so nobody made a big fuss about it. Right after class they simply wheeled out my charred corpse, and the next class walked in without so much as a blink. Scary School is a very strange place.

Much to my surprise, I came back as a ghost unable to leave the Scary School grounds. When you come back as a ghost, it means you still have something left to accomplish. For a long time, I couldn't figure out what that was, but then I remembered that I had always wanted to be a writer when I grew up. It occurred to me that no one had ever written about Scary School and all the horrible, wonderful things that go on there.

So this year, I floated around the school, writing down all the crazy things that happened on my ghost pad. My ghost pad never runs out of paper and my ghost pen never runs out of ink. It's pretty cool being a ghostwriter. It turned out that this year was an exciting year to write about. Scary School was chosen to host the annual Ghoul Games (more about this soon), making it the scariest year in Scary School history.

This page is a lot like a front door. As soon as you turn it, you'll be opening the front door to Scary School, and once you step in, there is no guarantee you will make it out alive. Good luck!

1

Charles, the New Kid

It's not often that a new kid arrives at Scary School, but when one does, no one wants to bother learning yet another name, so they just call him or her "new kid."

Everyone knows that the human brain can only hold so many names. About fifty is all there's room for. So every time you meet someone and learn a new name, someone else's name gets pushed out to make room for the new one. Whenever you see someone you haven't seen in a long time and you can't remember their name, that's what happened.

If you can remember more than fifty names, that means you have a superbrain and there's no excuse for not getting straight As.

Charles, a new kid, stood outside on the front lawn of Scary School. It looks like a perfectly normal school to me, he thought to himself. Nicely painted brown and yellow, two stories tall, a waving flag . . . nothing seems scary about this place at all.

They say not to judge a book by its cover. Charles shouldn't have judged Scary School by its exterior.

As Charles walked toward the front entrance of the school, he couldn't have been happier. He had heard Scary School was the hardest school in the world, and he liked a challenge. Charles didn't usually have a whole lot to be happy about. He was so skinny, the kids at his last school called him Toothpick. That was because his arms looked like two toothpicks and his legs looked like two toothpicks. Then, those four toothpicks were attached to a fifth toothpick called his body.

To make matters worse, his head was large and egg-shaped. Nobody understood how his toothpick

of a neck managed to hold it upright. Imagine trying to balance an egg on its narrow end—it should have just plopped over and cracked open.

At the school's front entrance, Charles came to a large, dark moat separating the school from the vast front lawn. There didn't seem to be any way across the moat, and since Charles had arrived more than a half hour early, there weren't any other kids around to show him how to get into the school.

Am I supposed to swim across? Charles thought to himself, scratching the shell of his perfectly combed hair, that didn't have a single strand out of

Charles, the New Kid

place. He looked at his watch. 7:29 a.m. He was determined to be the first student to enter the school and made a hasty decision he would very soon regret.

Charles dipped his toe into the moat and a giant, slimy tentacle shot out of the murky water and wrapped itself around Charles's leg. The tentacle began pulling him into the moat. Charles grabbed on to the grassy edge of the moat with all his strength.

Unfortunately, Charles was the furthest thing from strong and he was quickly yanked off the ground, flipped into the air, and deftly caught by another tentacle high above the water.

A towering pink figure that had a giant eye at least ten feet across rose from the moat.

"Oh my gosh!" screamed Charles. "An *Architeuthis*!"

Charles knew the scientific name for giant squid because nature programs were the only television programs his zoologist parents let him watch.

The giant squid squinted at Charles, squeezing him in his giant tentacle, licking his giant beak.

"You are going to taste sooo good," said the creature, drooling. "I am so sick of eating crab."

Then there was a loud roar, but not from the squid. A twenty-foot *Tyrannosaurus rex* wearing a blue dress and a blue bonnet stomped toward the moat.

"Archie! It's seven thirty," roared the dinosaur.

"Scary School is now open."

"Uh-oh," said Archie the giant squid, and a great drawbridge dropped down from the front wall and clonked Archie right on his giant pink head.

The impact knocked Charles loose from the squid's grip, and he flew through the air, landing on the snout of the *Tyrannosaurus rex* in a blue dress.

It seemed Charles was out of the frying pan and into the fire. "Are you going to eat me?" he nervously asked the T. rex.

"Luckily for you I already had breakfast," said the T. rex, in a nice old lady's voice. "And from the looks of you, you're going to have to keep getting lucky to survive here."

"I don't believe in luck," said Charles.

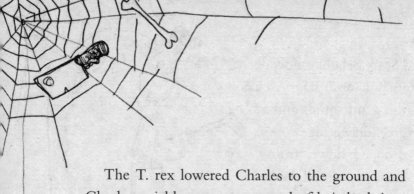

The T. rex lowered Charles to the ground and Charles quickly put every strand of hair back into place that had gone awry. Then a wave of students (that seemed to arrive out of nowhere) rushed past him and filled the entry hall of Scary School.

"Move along," said the T. rex in a blue dress. "If you're late you'll end up in my detention room, and I might get hungry again."

The locker hallway looked like a twisted, spooky maze with high rows of lockers that arched menacingly over the students below. Crevices, secret passageways, and trapdoors made navigating the hallway a particularly difficult task, but Charles followed a map that had been mailed to him in advance. He didn't know it, but he barely avoided getting eaten by Locker 39, the meanest locker of them all. There will be much more about Locker 39 in the next book.

As Charles walked down the hall, everyone was saying, "Hey, new kid," "Hey, new kid," "Hey, new kid," and he thought they were all being *very* friendly and calling him by his name, which happened to

be Charles Nukid. He didn't realize that all the kids were making fun of him and not being friendly at all.

The reason everyone knew Charles Nukid was a new kid was because he wasn't wearing the school uniform—or rather, he *was* wearing the school uniform.

Scary School has a very strict uniform policy that states, "The school uniform must be worn by all students at all times." The uniform consists of gray shorts, a white dress shirt, and a polka-dot tie.

The problem was, whenever a kid put on the uniform and looked in the mirror, they immediately saw how stupid they looked and refused to wear it. Every kid just went to school wearing whatever they wanted, but never wore gray shorts, a white dress shirt, or a polka-dot tie.

Because no one ever wore the Scary School uniform to school, none of the teachers even knew what it looked like, so they assumed that not wearing the school uniform *was* the school uniform. If a kid showed up wearing the school uniform (usually a new kid) the teachers all thought that kid must be out of uniform, and he got detention.

Because he was a new kid, Charles Nukid didn't know that not wearing the school uniform was the school uniform, and he showed up wearing the gray

Mr.
Spider~
Eyes

shorts, white dress shirt, and polka-dot tie.

The hallway monitor, Mr. Spider-Eyes, was the first to see Charles. Mr. Spider-Eyes has one hundred tiny eyes where most people have just one eye. Using normal math, that's two hundred eyes on his head, but using Monster Math that's over six thousand eyes. More about that later.

Mr. Spider-Eyes uses each one of his eyes to spy on every kid in the hallway at the same time. Having spotted Charles out of uniform, he shouted, "Hey, you! Get over here!"

Charles pointed to himself. "Me?"

"Yeah, you! Come here!"

Charles stepped nervously toward Mr. Spider-Eyes, not knowing what he was in trouble for before his first class even started.

"Just what do you think you're doing not wearing the school uniform?" Mr. Spider-Eyes inquired.

"But I am wearing the school uniform. Every bit of it," replied Charles.

"Oh, really? Do you see anyone else around here wearing gray shorts, a white dress shirt, and a polka-dot tie?"

Charles looked at all the kids in the hall, and of course no one was dressed like him.

"No," said Charles.

"Well then, how can it be the school uniform if no one is wearing it?"

"I don't know. It's my first day here."

"Oh, it's your first day! Well, that's no excuse. I suppose you wanted to make an impression and show everyone what a rule-breaking rebel you are, eh?"

"Me? No! I never break the rules. I like following the rules."

That was true. Nothing pleased Charles more than following the rules, no matter what they were. In fact, he always went to bed an hour early each night at 8:00 p.m., just to make sure he'd be asleep by his 9:00 p.m. bedtime. He thought if he was still awake after 9:00 p.m., that would be breaking the rules. He'd feel so guilty that he wouldn't sleep for a week, which would make him feel even guiltier, and he wouldn't be able to sleep for two more weeks, thus starting a horrible, sleepless cycle. Once when he was seven, Charles missed his bedtime, the cycle began, and he didn't sleep for a whole year.

"Oh, you like following rules, huh?" Mr. Spider-Eyes grunted. "Well, the rule at Scary School is that you can't go to class if you're not in uniform. You'll have to go straight to the detention hall and stay there until you're wearing the school uniform."

"Okay, I guess I made a mistake," said Charles, bewildered. "I'm happy to follow the rules and will go straight to the detention hall."

So instead of going to his fifth-grade class with Dr. Dragonbreath, Charles Nukid marched straight to the detention hall. He opened the door and was greeted by the same *Tyrannosaurus rex* wearing the blue dress and cute matching bonnet.

"Hello again, dear," said the dinosaur in her very sweet, old lady's voice. "Looks like you didn't get very lucky after all. I'm Mrs. T, the detention monitor. I see you're not wearing the school uniform."

"I know. I thought this was the uniform."

"No. That, my dear, is the furthest thing from the uniform."

"Well, what is the uniform?"

"I'm not sure. Anything but gray shorts, a white dress shirt, and a polka-dot tie, I suppose. Nobody *ever* wears *that*."

"But this is all I have with me."

"That's too bad. The rule is, you have to stay in detention until you are wearing the proper uniform."

"Okay, then that's what I'll do."

"Of course," continued Mrs. T, "if you were to leave and go get the right uniform from your house, I would certainly understand."

"But that would be breaking the rules," said Charles.

"Yes, but I sympathize with your situation, and I certainly wouldn't do anything to stop you."

"No," said Charles. "I can't break the rules. I will stay here until I am wearing the correct uniform."

"Very well," said Mrs. T, "but just to warn you, I get very hungry around lunchtime. I may not be able to control myself and I will most likely eat you at noon."

"But, isn't eating students against the rules?" Charles asked hopefully.

"Yes, indeed. But I'm a dinosaur, my dear. Breaking the rules doesn't bother me."

I know things seem hopeless for Charles, but in Chapter Six you'll see how he manages a very lucky escape!

2

Ms. Fang

Ms. Fang is the nicest, sweetest teacher at Scary School. She only ate twelve kids last year.

Her fifth-grade class knew they were very lucky to have her. The other fifth-grade class had Dr. Dragonbreath. Last year he ate his entire class on the first day and got to spend the rest of the year on paid vacation.

Ms. Fang's class called her Ms. Fang because she has one big fang on the right side of her mouth. If she had two fangs like most vampires, they would call her Ms. Fangs.

Her real name is Ms. Fangleheimershratzenpfeffer. It's a very common name in Transylvania.

The first day of class, Ms. Fang told the class her full name, but said they could call her Ms. Fangs for short. She wrote *Ms. Fangs* on the chalkboard. Benny Porter, a chubby kid with spiky hair, raised his hand. Benny's nickname was Benny the Bruiser because he liked to give kids bruises by socking them on the arm or leg.

Benny said with a smirk, "But you only have *one* fang, Ms. Fangs. Shouldn't we call you Ms. *Fang*?" He laughed and tried to high-five the boy next to him, but the boy very smartly left him hanging.

Benny had angered Ms. Fang because she was quite embarrassed about having just one fang. She lost her second fang in a tragic checkers accident, but we'll get to that later.

After Benny asked that question, Ms. Fang's pale white skin turned beet red. She pounced on Benny and sucked out all his blood with only one fang, so it took twice as long as normal. When she was done, she dropped Benny on the floor, where he lay motionless, drained of blood.

"Anyone else care to spread lies about my fangs?" she asked.

No one said a word.

She turned around and walked back to her desk, but then stopped dead in her tracks. She turned back around, felt inside her mouth, and said, "Oh my goodness. I *do* only have one fang. I completely forgot. What Benny said makes total sense now. I'm soooo sorry, Benny. Will you please forgive me?"

Benny, of course, did not answer her because he was dead.

Okay, before we go on, allow me to explain a few

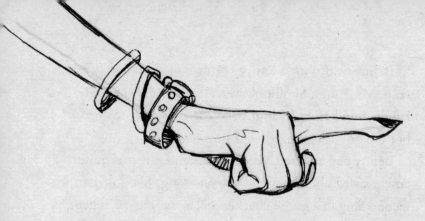

things. You're probably thinking this book isn't going to be very wholesome at all. Well, don't worry; just because a kid dies at Scary School, it doesn't mean that he or she will stay dead. As you will see, there's all sorts of ways a kid can come back from the dead and keep attending classes. In fact, losing your life is *never* an excuse for missing class. Plus, through the act of dying, a dead student will ironically learn an important life lesson. It is such life lessons that will make Scary School probably the most wholesome book series to be published in the last twenty years.

Okay, kids, that last part was just for your parents and teachers. Between you and me, if that mean kid in your class got bitten by a vampire, it would be pretty funny, right? I know I was laughing when I saw it happen. Back to the classroom . . .

Ms. Fang looked down with regret at Benny's pasty corpse. "You don't have to say anything, Benny. Just know that I'm very sorry."

Ms. Fang was definitely the nicest teacher at Scary School. How many teachers have you ever seen apologize to one of their students after they'd been mean?

Ms. Fang erased the *s* from her name on the chalkboard so that it now read *Ms. Fang*.

"I want all of you to call me Ms. Fang from now on," she said, "in honor of Benny's memory." Ms. Fang pointed to Wendy Crumkin, a very smart girl with glasses and freckles.

Wendy

"Wendy," asked Ms. Fang, "what are you going to call me from now on?"

Because Wendy was so smart, she had taken note of what had happened to Benny Porter when he called the teacher Ms. Fang, so she said, "Ms. Fangs, of course."

Once again, Ms. Fang became very angry, and her pale skin turned an even deeper shade of red than before.

"How dare you disobey me!" she shrieked. Then she pounced on Wendy and sucked out all of her blood.

Wendy dropped dead on the floor.

"Class," Ms. Fang huffed, her mouth dripping with blood, "what are you going to call me?"

"Ms. Fang!" they all proclaimed in unison.

"Excellent," she said, satisfied. "Now we can begin our lesson in geography. And Wendy, I'm sorry I had to make an example of you."

Wendy did not answer her as she was dead now as well.

Okay, there wasn't much of a life lesson to be learned there, but I guess sometimes bad things just happen for no good reason, and that's an important lesson in itself.

As soon as class ended, the three Rachels ran to the front of the class and pushed a big red button next to the doorway, which sent an alert to Nurse Hairymoles that something was wrong.

"Do you think Nurse Hairymoles will be able to save them?" Rachael asked Raychel.

"I don't know," said Raychel. "They've been dead for almost an hour. She would have to be one heck of a good nurse."

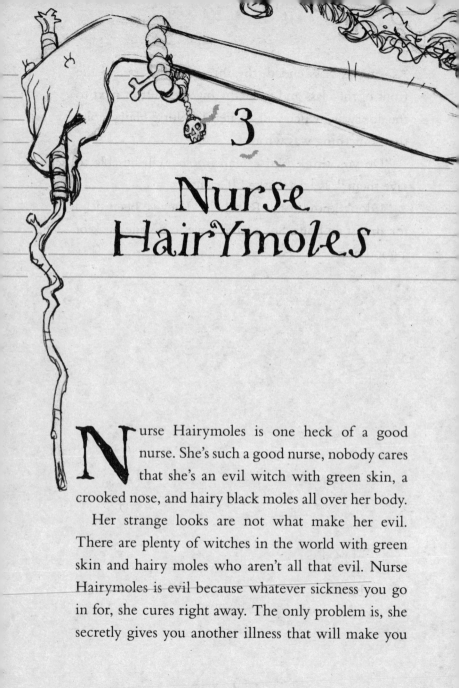

3
Nurse Hairymoles

Nurse Hairymoles is one heck of a good nurse. She's such a good nurse, nobody cares that she's an evil witch with green skin, a crooked nose, and hairy black moles all over her body.

Her strange looks are not what make her evil. There are plenty of witches in the world with green skin and hairy moles who aren't all that evil. Nurse Hairymoles is evil because whatever sickness you go in for, she cures right away. The only problem is, she secretly gives you another illness that will make you

even sicker the next day, so
you have to go back to see
her again. Then she cures that
problem and gives you a brand-
new one. Her nursing business is
very successful because of this.

Everyone thinks Nurse Hairymoles
is the best nurse in the world, which is true,
because she can cure absolutely anything. What nurse
do you know who can do that? But everything always

evens out in life, so her miraculous nursing talent is balanced by her nasty tendency to make you even sicker with brand-new maladies. There's a good saying on how to deal with this type of person in your life: *you take the good with the bad.*

After Ms. Fang's first class ended, the three Rachels pushed the big red button next to the doorway and swiftly fell through a trapdoor that had opened beneath their feet. After sliding down a long tube, the Rachels dropped into the middle of Nurse Hairymoles's office. None of the three Rachels spell their name *Rachel.* One is Rachael, one is Raychel, and one is Frank, which is pronounced "Rachel." The kids speculate that Frank's parents don't know how to read, but more about that later.

The three Rachels—Rachael, Raychel, and Frank—shouted, "Come quick! Ms. Fang bit two kids an hour ago!"

"Don't you mean *Ms. Fangs?*" asked Nurse Hairymoles.

"No, it's *Ms. Fang* now. And don't call her *Ms. Fangs* anymore or she'll bite you, too."

Nurse Hairymoles waved her magic wand, and in a flash, she and the three Rachels appeared in the classroom in a cloud of smoke. All the smoke made it hard to find Benny and Wendy, but eventually, Rachael and Frank tripped over their lifeless bodies on the floor and called Nurse Hairymoles to them.

Nurse Hairymoles pulled the two dead kids and the three Rachels together, waved her wand, and zapped everyone back to her office.

Inside it looked more like a haunted laboratory than a nurse's office. There were cages of newts, lizards, and giant bugs. Tanks of sea slugs, piranhas, and eels. Beakers of slime, sludge, and muck.

Nurse Hairymoles did a quick examination of Benny and Wendy.

"These kids have had all the blood sucked out of them!" Nurse Hairymoles exclaimed.

"Well, duh," said Rachael and Raychel.

"Can you cure them?" asked Frank, which is pronounced "Rachel."

"Of course I can," Nurse Hairymoles said, "but I only have enough blood in storage to save one of them. The other one is going to need new blood from someone else."

Nurse Hairymoles opened a refrigerator in the room and pulled out what looked like a plastic milk carton filled with blood. She poked one end of her magic wand into the milk carton and put the other end on Benny's arm. Soon Benny filled up with blood, just like a balloon being blown

BLOOD TRANSFUSION!

up. All his color came back, and he opened his eyes.

The three Rachels cheered.

"I'm alive!" Benny shouted. "Thank you, Nurse Hairymoles!" And he gave her a big kiss on her crooked green nose covered with hairy moles.

"Here," said Nurse Hairymoles, holding out her hand with a purple pill in it. "Take this pill to get your strength back." Benny took the pill (which secretly contained a vicious flu virus) and skipped out of the room, leaving behind the still-lifeless Wendy.

"Wellll," croaked Nurse Hairymoles, "which one of you girls wants to donate all your blood so I can bring Wendy back to life?"

"But, if you take our blood, won't we die?" asked Raychel, quivering.

"Of course you will. But as you've seen, I can bring you right back to life as long as I can get someone else's blood."

"I see," said Raychel. "Rachael, will you give me your blood after I die?"

"Of course. You're my best friend, Raychel. I'd be happy to give you my blood."

So Nurse Hairymoles put one end of her wand on Raychel's arm and the other end on Wendy's arm. Wendy filled up just like a balloon, opened her eyes, took her pill, and skipped away happily.

Raychel dropped dead on the floor.

Then Rachael stepped forward, and the process was repeated. Raychel came back to life, skipped away, and then Rachael dropped dead.

That left Frank, which is pronounced "Rachel," in case you forgot.

"Well, Frank. Do you want to save Raychel's life?" asked Nurse Hairymoles.

"To be honest, I don't really like either of the Rachels. They always make fun of how my name is spelled. But . . . I suppose it's the right thing to do."

So Frank gave her blood to Rachael, who came back to life and skipped away.

At this point, there was no more blood left for Frank. Nurse Hairymoles sounded a loud alarm, and all the kids at Scary School lined up at her office. Frank's best friend, Petunia, gave her blood to Frank, and then Johnny, who had a crush on Petunia, gave his blood to Petunia. On and on it went until every kid at Scary School had given their blood to someone else. Each had saved someone's life, dropped dead, and come back to life.

Unfortunately, Benny Porter had to run to the bathroom after coming back to life and did not hear the alarm because he was making even louder noises in the bathroom stall.

By the time Benny got out and realized what was happening, he was the last in line. When it finally came to him, Benny gave his blood to Jason and dropped dead once again. That was the second time Benny had died that day. How many people can say that's ever happened to them?

Even more unfortunately, since there was no one left in line, no one was obligated to give Benny more blood. No one really liked Benny so no one volunteered, and the kids went about their normal school day as poor Benny lay dead once again on Nurse Hairymoles's floor.

Principal Headcrusher walked in to assess the

Vampire
Benny

situation. "Well," she said, "Scary School policy states that if a student gets drained of his blood and there's no more blood left to save him, then he must be turned into a vampire."

"Ugh, that's not my job, is it?" groaned Nurse Hairymoles.

"No, Nurse Hairymoles. His parents will have to find their own Turner that will suit him best."

"Thank goodness," said Nurse Hairymoles, "because I have a hot date tonight."

Principal Headcrusher's jaw dropped. She did a terrible job of hiding her shock.

"Riiight," Principal Headcrusher said, forcing a smile. "Well, it's a stupid rule if you ask me. Deceased students would be so much more useful as food for the Venus flytraps, wouldn't you say?"

"Yes, Principal Headcrusher."

"But you know how parents are these days, what with wanting to keep their kids alive. Pfff. Whatever."

And so Benny got to stay home from Scary School for a whole week while he was being turned into a vampire. Then he got to stay home another week while he suffered from a vicious flu.

All the kids were jealous.

4

Principal
Headcrusher

Two weeks into the year, Scary School had settled into a normal routine. At 7:30 a.m., Principal Headcrusher unlocked the school gates, made a cup of coffee, and entered her office expecting another predictable day of learning, horror, and mayhem. Instead, she found an envelope sitting on her desk with a seal that said *ISG*.

Principal Headcrusher dropped her coffee and began trembling.

"This is it," she said to herself, so excited she was frozen in place. She slowly picked up the envelope,

Principal
Headcrusher

opened it very, very carefully using her teeth (since her hands were far too big and clumsy), and read these words:

Dear Principal Meredith Headcrusher of Scary School,

We received your application and are very pleased to inform you that Scary School has been selected to host this year's Ghoul Games.
  More information and surprise visits to follow.

  Sincerely,
  Franz Dietrich Wolfbark
  Ghoul Games Committee Chairman,
  International Society of Ghouls

Upon reading this letter, Principal Headcrusher did a dance of joy around her office that I dare not describe to you, for it would be the scariest thing I've yet written and would give you nightmares for the rest of your life. Some people shouldn't dance.

The students and faculty were immediately called into a special assembly in Petrified Pavilion.

Petrified Pavilion is a structure of uncommon beauty and gothic eeriness. Constructed completely from petrified wood, it looks as if a great tree has magically risen from the ground in the form of a glorious spherical hall. Though the exterior resembles tree bark, it shines like polished marble. The enormous spherical face of the structure looks like the face of a man, literally petrified in an eternal scream.

Through the open mouth of the screaming face is the school gymnasium and grand hall, but to enter the hall is no simple task. The open mouth of the screaming face is hundreds of feet in the air. In order to gain

entry, students and faculty must stand together on gigantic branches that hang loosely on the tree's side like wooden hands the size of buses. Once students are standing on the hands, permission to enter is verified and Petrified Pavilion lifts its hands toward its mouth, and the students must quickly hop off into the grand hall. From a distance, it appears as though the pavilion is eating its entrants alive.

To make matters worse, perched upon the head of the pavilion are gargoyles, and not the fake stone kinds you're used to seeing. These are real gargoyles with leathery wings, sharp teeth, and horns. They perch patiently, waiting for naughty kids to try to enter the pavilion when they're not supposed to.

The gargoyles have been known to fly down and snatch up kids if they get hungry or bored, but they're only *supposed* to snatch kids who break the rules and try to sneak into Petrified Pavilion without a teacher. Some of the kids have thought of ingenious plans to get past the gargoyles and enter the pavilion without being snatched up and eaten. It's even a rite of passage for one of Scary School's secret clubs, but more about that in future books.

At 8:05 a.m., all the kids and teachers were piled into the bleachers of Petrified Pavilion for the special announcement. When Principal Headcrusher stepped up to the podium and announced that Scary School would be hosting this year's Ghoul Games, she was expecting the pavilion to burst into thunderous applause and cheers. But there was complete silence.

The awkward silence continued for several minutes as everyone sat on their hands staring at Principal Headcrusher while she stared back at them. Nobody knew if what she said was good news or bad news. They were afraid to react the wrong way, which would most certainly entice Principal Headcrusher to reach out and crush their heads.

Eventually, Benny Porter, who had just come back to school as a child vampire, raised his hand.

"Yes, we have a question?" said Principal Headcrusher.

"Principal Headcrusher, what are the Ghoul Games?" Benny asked.

Everyone let out a big sigh of relief as the tension was snapped.

"Really? None of you have heard of the Ghoul Games?"

Everyone shook their heads.

"Well, it's very good news," she said.

Everyone burst into thunderous applause and cheers.

"Yes, yes, it's very exciting. The Ghoul Games is the biggest event of the year for all the scary creatures of the world. They will be coming to our school to compete against us in many kinds of games. Every student will have to pick a game to compete in against the other ghouls, goblins, and monsters. That's right, *each one of you* must participate in a game of your choice. But the reason this is so historic is because this is the *first time* human children have been allowed to participate in the Ghoul Games. It means our school has finally been recognized as part of the Scary community!"

"What games do we play?" asked Jason. "Do we play hockey?"

"I told you," said Principal Headcrusher. "You can play any kind of game you want—sports games, video games, board games, mind games, blame games . . . you name it."

Charles Nukid smiled very broadly when he heard he could play video games. He had been playing Guitar Legend all alone in his room for years and was pretty sure he was the best in the world at it, but never had a chance to show anyone.

Principal Headcrusher continued, "The Games will begin in the spring, so you have the whole school year to prepare. Plus, the school that wins the Ghoul Games receives a Golden Elephant and gets to go on a trip to Albania to meet the Monster King! Assembly dismissed."

As the kids walked back to class, they couldn't contain their excitement. They were all trying to figure out what game they were going to play in the Ghoul Games. Sign-ups were just a week away.

"I'm going to play basketball," said Johnny.

"I'm going to play hopscotch," said Lindsey.

"I'm going to play dead," said Penny Possum.

For some it was an easy choice, but for most, they weren't sure what they were best at and had to do some serious thinking.

Charles Nukid couldn't wait for spring to arrive. He would finally get to show off his video game guitar skills to the whole school. It gave him a real sense of purpose he hadn't felt before. Maybe I'll dye my hair green for the added effect, he thought to himself. Then he shook his head, thinking, nah, that might be against the rules.

Principal Headcrusher stood in the hall smiling as she

held her giant hands against her ears and eavesdropped on all the kids' conversations about the Ghoul Games. It was what she'd been waiting for her whole life.

When she was born, Principal Headcrusher's parents did not know what to make of her. How could a baby's hands be as big as her body and as strong as a gorilla's? Worse, she had no control of her strength in her first few years of life. She almost crushed her own parents' heads so many times that they had to walk around the house wearing football helmets. Bottles were impossible, because when she squeezed one, it would immediately explode, sending milk flying everywhere.

Baby
Headcrusher

The doctors all said she was a perfectly normal little girl except for those hands, so when she was old enough to start school, her parents faced a very hard decision. On one hand, the little Headcrusher needed to go to school and make friends. On the other hand, they certainly didn't want their daughter to accidentally (or purposefully) crush the heads of other kids or teachers. That wouldn't go over well at a regular school.

Her parents' prayers were answered on a summer morning when they opened the door and an abominable snowman was standing there. He introduced himself as Rolf, and told them he was the principal of Scream Academy (also known as the Aaaaaah!cademy). He offered young Meredith Headcrusher a place in his school, which was hidden deep in the arctic mountains. This was a great honor, as she would become the first human child to attend the same school as monsters, vampires, werewolves, zombies, dragons, and ghosts.

At first things were very hard for Meredith at the Aaaaaah!cademy. No one wanted to be her friend because she was so different—not because of her hands, but because she was a human, and humans had never been very nice to monsters, dragons, and other scary creatures in the past. Then, one day, the nastiest bully at the school, Tony the troll, pushed Meredith to the ground and tried to steal her lunch money. When

Tony got close enough, she socked him in the jaw, and Tony stumbled back in shock.

Infuriated, Tony rushed toward her, growling and drooling, about to gobble her up, but Meredith instinctively reached out and crushed the troll's head before he could eat her. Tony the troll learned a very valuable life lesson about not bullying little girls with enormous hands.

When the other kids saw what had happened, they hoisted Meredith up on their shoulders and carried her around the school chanting her name. "Headcrusher! Headcrusher! Headcrusher!" They were so glad that the bully was gone, Meredith became the school hero and was even elected class president.

From that point forward, Meredith was very happy at Scream Academy. When she'd go back home for the summer, she'd tell all the kids on her block about her scary school, and they were all jealous that she got to go to a school that was never, ever boring.

By far, Principal Headcrusher's favorite thing about Scream Academy was the Ghoul Games—the annual competition in various games between all the Scary schools on Earth. Young Meredith won the trophy for arm wrestling every single year. There was always a big crowd to watch her arm wrestle, and Scary students from competing schools would hoot and holler as she took down beasts and monsters five times her size with ease.

Meredith Headcrusher went on to teach human history at Scream Academy for many years before moving back to the United States to found Scary School—the first and only school to mix regular kids with Scary kids and Scary teachers. At last, her students were going to have the same opportunity she'd had as a young student to meet monsters from all over the world and possibly even attain glory and acclaim through victory.

But most importantly, an invitation to the Ghoul Games meant that Scary School was finally being recognized as a success. Nobody ever thought in a million years that there could be a functioning school mixing monsters and humans, but not only was it functioning, it was succeeding beyond her wildest dreams.

If the Ghoul Games went well, it could spell an end to the thousands of years of human-monster separation, which had been Principal Headcrusher's highest aspiration from the moment she decided to open Scary School.

Principal Headcrusher reentered her office at 8:30 a.m. practically dancing on air, only to trip and fall at the feet of a thin man in a drab gray suit. His face was sunken in, almost skeletal. He wore thin-framed glasses and his stringy gray hair was slicked back on his spotty head.

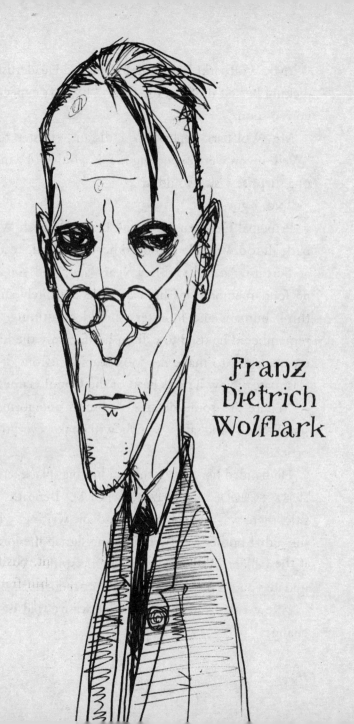

Franz
Dietrich
Wolfbark

"Mr. Wolfbark!" exclaimed Principal Headcrusher, picking herself up from the floor. "I wasn't expecting you so soon."

Mr. Wolfbark replied in a distant, sinister tone, "Well, if you were expecting me, it wouldn't be much of a surprise visit, would it?"

"No, I guess not."

Principal Headcrusher knew Franz Dietrich Wolfbark all too well. He had been her fifth-grade teacher at Scream Academy thirty years ago, and she had *no* fond memories of his class. He definitely didn't think humans and monsters should be mixing. She remembered he used to call on her for only the hardest questions to make her look stupid in front of her classmates. Now he was head of the Ghoul Games.

"There are some details to discuss and forms to sign," Wolfbark said, "which will make everything official."

He handed her a form that said in big, black letters, HOST SCHOOL ACCEPTANCE FORM. Beneath that title, there was a bunch of microscopic writing, which she didn't bother to read before she signed the form.

"Excellent," he said with a cagey smile. "Now to update you on the new rules and procedures."

"New rules and procedures? I wasn't told of any changes."

"Of course you didn't think it would remain exactly the same with humans in the mix? Before this, you were the only human to ever compete in the Ghoul Games, and let's just say, you had a 'handy' advantage that these human children won't have, so some changes had to be made."

"Okay, what are the changes?"

"For the most part things will remain the same. Since you are the host school, your students will get to decide the games that will be played, and the other schools will send over their participants for each game. However, rather than awarding medals, the prizes will be quite different. You see, this year, the winners get to . . . eat . . . the losers."

Franz Wolfbark savored saying those last words and practically licked his chops at the thought of it.

"*What?*" Principal Headcrusher exclaimed. "But that means if the monsters win all the games, I won't have any more students. That would be the end of Scary School!"

"Yes, indeed. It will be the end of something that never should have existed in the first place. On the bright side, I'm sure the Scary kids who attend your school will be able to defend themselves and won't be eaten. I suppose it's only the human students who will be devoured, so in the end, you'll have a normal

Scary-community school just like all the others. And won't that be nice?"

Principal Headcrusher finally understood what was going on. Scary School wasn't chosen for the Ghoul Games to put it on the map, it was chosen to wipe it off the map.

"Mr. Wolfbark, please. It's one thing to lose a few students here and there to keep everyone on their toes, but I can't lose my entire paying student body. Besides, my kids won't even want to eat the monsters if they win."

"Don't worry. If the human students don't want to eat the monsters, they will be given lollipops instead. It's all on the acceptance form you just signed and agreed to. Feel free to take a closer look at your copy."

It took all of Principal Headcrusher's willpower not to crush Franz Wolfbark's head right there.

"Farewell, Principal Headcrusher. If I don't see you the next full moon, then certainly this spring." There was a burst of smoke around Wolfbark. When the smoke cleared, Wolfbark was still standing there. He started whistling and walked out the office door rather unremarkably. Principal Headcrusher scratched her head in confusion. Suddenly, the smoke alarm went off, ceiling sprinklers popped out, and her entire office was drenched in streams of water.

Dripping wet, Principal Headcrusher seethed as Wolfbark laughed like a hyena from the hallway.

5

Fred, the Boy Without Fear

Everyone loves Fred because he is the school hero.

The morning after the special assembly, Principal Headcrusher announced on the PA system that there were new rules to the Ghoul Games and that Scary School students would be eaten alive by the monsters if they lost. Every student in the classroom yelped at the same time, except for Fred.

Growing up, Fred had terrifying nightmares about monsters and ghouls every night and would wake up screaming at the top of his lungs. His parents would rush in and tell him over and over that there was no such thing as monsters—that it was all just a dream.

His parents were very convincing, and Fred was certain that the monsters that plagued his dreams didn't really exist.

Therefore, when Fred started at Scary School and began seeing the creatures from his nightmares everywhere he looked, he naturally assumed he must be dreaming. Because Fred always thought he was dreaming whenever he was at school, he didn't think anything he saw was real, so he was never afraid. He was the boy without fear.

When Dr. Dragonbreath walked down

Fred

the hallway, all the kids scattered against the walls and dared not even look at him, but Fred would walk right past him and say, "Good morning!" with a smile. One time he even said, "Good morning, you big ugly dragon." Dr. Dragonbreath was furious, but he couldn't eat any kid who wasn't in his class and just stormed away fuming fire.

The kids thought Fred was either very brave or had a death wish, but Fred just thought nothing bad could possibly happen to him because it was all just a dream.

Another time, Fred witnessed a werewolf Scary kid named Peter push Jason to the ground after hockey practice. It looked like Peter the Wolf was about to rip Jason apart, so Fred fearlessly jumped into the fray. Fred got scratched up pretty badly, but he fought Peter off and Peter scampered away with his werewolf tail between his legs.

"Thank you, Fred," said Jason.

"Anytime," said Fred. "Boy, these cuts sure do feel real."

Jason looked at him strangely. But they were best friends after that.

Fred also started growing his fingernails long after his fight with Peter so that he wouldn't be at such a disadvantage if he ever had to fight Peter again.

However, the reason why Fred is the school hero is because of what happened in Mr. Acidbath's class last year. At the time, Fred was sitting with the rest of the fourth-grade class taking a spelling test. Their teacher, Mr. Rockface, was saying the words out loud and the class was writing them down.

"The final word is . . . explosion. Ex-plo-sion."

At that very moment, there was a loud explosion down the hall. *Kaboom!*

Everyone dropped their pencils and ran out of the room to see what had happened.

Across the hall, Mr. Acidbath's science classroom was a fiery inferno. Orange and blue flames were leaping out of the doorway. Mr. Acidbath and all his students were trapped inside screaming for help. I know because I, Derek the Ghost (before I was a ghost), was one of those students. I never thought I'd find out what it's like to be cooked inside an oven, but I was finding out at that moment.

Nurse Hairymoles and several teachers tried to bring in the Scary School fire hose to put out the fire, but it wasn't long enough to reach the classroom. No one had the courage to run in and try to save the students, and with good reason. The fire was so out of control that anyone who dared enter couldn't possibly make it out alive.

The only one who wasn't scared was Fred. As he watched the fire blazing before him, he was thinking, wow, this is such a vivid, realistic dream. I can really feel the heat from the flames.

Before anyone could hold him back, Fred dashed inside the classroom to rescue his schoolmates.

When he got inside, he saw dozens of kids rolling on the floor trying to put out the flames on their clothes. Fred seemed completely unaffected by the fire—it wasn't hurting him one bit. I know this is a dream, Fred thought to himself. If this were real, I would have been burned alive by now.

What Fred didn't know was that the fire had started when Mr. Acidbath's experiment with Fear Gas went terribly wrong and exploded. Because it was a Fear Gas fire, the flames were enchanted and would not hurt anyone who wasn't afraid. All the students, and even Mr. Acidbath, were terrified. The fire, feeding off their fear, was consuming them. But Fred, the boy without fear, repelled the flames like opposing magnets.

When Fred approached each of his schoolmates, the flames leaped off of them like frightened mice running away from a cat. One by one, he pulled each kid out of the fire, wrapped in a cocoon of fearless safety.

When he was finished, he had saved the lives of

twenty-two kids and Mr. Acidbath, who bore the brunt of the explosion and would have to take a leave of absence. Some kids were burned pretty badly, but it was nothing Nurse Hairymoles couldn't fix in a jiffy.

The only kid who didn't make it out alive was me. I thought I was being smart and jumped into the chemical cabinet, but I got locked inside and was cooked alive. Oops. I certainly learned a very important life lesson about what *not* to do in a fire.

Out in the hallway, everyone was cheering for Fred. The boys gave him high fives, the girls hugged him, and the teachers applauded.

"This is the best dream *ever*!" Fred shouted.

No one dared tell him it wasn't a dream, for fear of losing their school hero.

So, when Principal Headcrusher announced that the students would be eaten alive if they lost during the Ghoul Games, now you know why Fred was the only kid who wasn't afraid.

Jason whispered to him, "I'm definitely playing hockey now. What are you going to play, Fred?"

"Hmm. How about a deep-sleeping contest? Because I cannot seem to wake up no matter how hard I pinch myself."

6

Dr. Dragonbreath's Rules

In case you've been thinking that nothing all that
scary has happened yet, I am now going to take
you back to the first day of school. I didn't want to
tell you about Dr. Dragonbreath at the beginning of
the book because it may well have scared you off far
too soon. But now that you understand how Scary
School works and because you've proven yourself
to be very brave by reading this far, I think you're
ready to hear about what happened on the first day

of school in Dr. Dragonbreath's class.

At 8:00 a.m. on the first day, there were thirty kids in Dr. Dragonbreath's class.

At 8:12 a.m. on the first day, there were only two kids in Dr. Dragonbreath's class.

Principal Headcrusher was familiar with Dr. Dragonbreath's unusual teaching method, which tended not to support the more common notion that students should stay alive during class. Thus, Principal Headcrusher did not place any of the prized Scary kids in his class.

All thirty kids were in the classroom five minutes before class started. Some were nervous. Some were very nervous. Some were acting cool and relaxed, as if they didn't believe the horrible stories they had heard about Dr. Dragonbreath. A few were even misbehaving already, throwing spitballs and chasing one another around the room. Those ones definitely didn't believe the stories.

At precisely 8:00 a.m., Dr. Dragonbreath entered the classroom.

All loud noises and whispers turned to dead quiet.

Dr. Dragonbreath's name did not just describe his foul breath. He was, in fact, a nine-foot-tall dragon and he was all business. He walked upright on two thick legs and had strong arms with six-inch razor-sharp claws on each hand. He wore a perfectly ironed suit and tie over his green dragon scales, and wore thick black glasses on top of his long dragon snout. He never smiled, but when he spoke, it was clear that his teeth were designed for only one thing—eating fresh meat.

"Be seated," Dr. Dragonbreath said matter-of-factly, with the voice of an educated young scholar instead of a fearsome dragon.

The two kids who had frozen in place while running around the room quickly returned to their seats. Dr. Dragonbreath set down a black briefcase on his desk and addressed the class.

"Hello, I am Dr. Dragonbreath. I have a PhD in dragon history and lore, not medicine, so don't ask me to cure your sniffles unless you have no interest in keeping your various appendages."

The students' mouths hung open in silence.

"As you may have heard, many students have not survived my class in the past, but I sincerely hope that things will be different with you. All you have to do to survive is follow a very simple list of rules called 'Dr. Dragonbreath's Rules.' If you disobey any of the rules, the consequences will be immediate and fatal."

The kids looked at one another and gulped.

"Ah, see!" growled Dr. Dragonbreath. "Most of you just broke one of the rules by taking your attention off of me and looking at each other. *But*, since you didn't know that rule yet, you will be forgiven this one time. You see, I'm tough, but fair. These, my young pupils, are Dr. Dragonbreath's Rules."

Dr. Dragonbreath pulled a large scroll of paper down from the ceiling. On it was written a list of five rules in dark red ink that may very well have been blood.

"These are the five rules of my class, numbered one through five. The order of the rules does not indicate the importance of one rule over another, as failure to follow any of the rules will be equally catastrophic for you."

The kids gulped again, but kept staring straight ahead.

Dr. Dragonbreath continued, "As I point to each rule, please read that rule quietly to yourself." Dr. Dragonbreath extended one of his razor-sharp claws and pointed to . . .

RULE NUMBER ONE. ALWAYS RAISE YOUR HAND BEFORE SPEAKING.

"Simple enough, right? I'm sure that's been a rule in all of your classes."

Cindy Chan, one of the nervous kids, raised her hand.

"Look, everyone! Someone is already using Rule

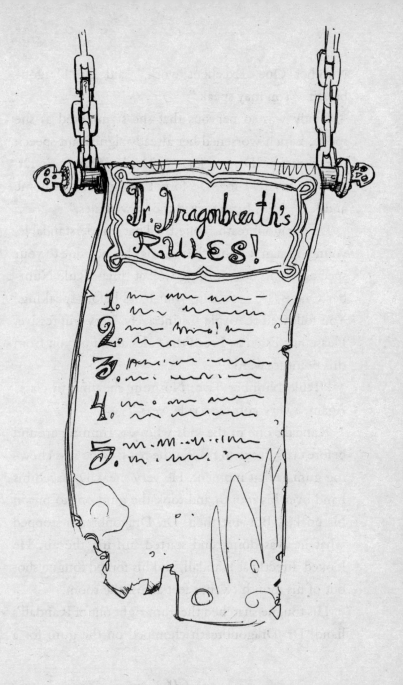

Dr. Dragonbreath's
RULES!

1.
2.
3.
4.
5.

Number One. Excellent work," said Dr. Dragon-breath. "You may speak."

Cindy was so nervous that she stammered as she spoke, which worsened her already significant speech impediment. "Dr. . . . Dr. . . . Dr. . . . Dwag . . . Dr. Dwagonbweff, I for . . . forgot my gwasses at home and I . . . I . . . I can't wead the w-w-wules."

Dr. Dragonbreath replied, "That's understandable, young human. I know these things happen due to your species's brain not working well at times. Rule Number One is, 'Always raise your hand before speaking.' You followed that rule instinctively. Very impressive. Please just listen as I read the rules aloud to you from this point forward."

"'Rule Number Two. No gum chewing in class.' Again, a very common rule, yes?"

Randall, one of the kids who was running around before class, froze in place as he realized he was chewing gum at that moment. He very sneakily placed his hand over his mouth and took the gum out to put in his pocket. But just then, Dr. Dragonbreath stopped what he was doing and started sniffing the air. He looked directly at Randall, and his forked tongue shot out of his mouth twenty feet across the room.

His tongue snatched the gum right out of Randall's hand! Dr. Dragonbreath chomped on the gum for a few seconds before blowing an enormous bubble filled with *dragon breath*. Dragon breath is a combination of air and fire, so when he spit out the bubble, it floated around the room like a glowing hot-air balloon.

The kids gaped in awe. When the bubble floated back to him, Dr. Dragonbreath popped it with his claw, and it exploded in a marvelous ball of fire before vanishing. The kids cried, "Hurrah!" and cheered their hearts out.

"Thank you," said Dr. Dragonbreath, taking a bow. "See, just because there are strict rules, that doesn't mean class can't be fun. And fear not, Randall. You did not know that rule before you were chewing, so you are excused this one time. I'm tough, but fair.

"'Rule Number Three. Your full attention must be given to Dr. Dragonbreath or to the work at hand at all times.' Again, no different from your other classes, only here, the consequences are far more severe. Earlier, when you turned your heads away from me and looked at one another, you were not giving me your full attention, and thus were breaking Rule Number Three."

All the kids kept their necks perfectly straight and did not move an inch.

"'Rule Number Four. Cartwheels, backflips, front flips, or incredible gymnastic routines of any kind are not allowed during class.'"

The class stared at Dr. Dragonbreath in silence, a bit confused. Was this a problem in his previous classes? they were all thinking.

"That rule is what you humans call a 'joke.' It is there for the sole purpose of making you laugh," said Dr. Dragonbreath, still not smiling. "You see, I wouldn't expect any of you to actually do a gymnastic routine during class. For one thing, there isn't enough space with all the desks."

No one was laughing.

"I suppose I'll never understand human humor," he grumbled. "Lastly is Rule Number Five. Now, I must warn you, this is the rule that my students always seem to have the most trouble following, which inevitably leads to their demise. Does anyone have any last words?"

No one spoke, for fear of breaking Rule Number One.

"Excellent job, class!" proclaimed Dr. Dragonbreath. "I thought for sure someone would break Rule Number One. I am indeed impressed. So, without any further ado, I give you . . . Rule Number Five."

Dr. Dragonbreath pointed to Rule Number Five without saying a word. Almost all of the students followed his claw and instinctively read the rule to themselves. Here is what it said:

RULE NUMBER FIVE. THIS IS THE FORBIDDEN RULE. NO STUDENT IS ALLOWED TO READ THIS SENTENCE.

With his keen dragon eyes enhanced all the more by his magical dragon glasses, Dr. Dragonbreath took mental note of every single student who was reading Rule Number Five and therefore breaking Rule Number Five.

After reading the rule, all the students looked up at Dr. Dragonbreath nervously. He took off his glasses, loosened his tie, and smiled for the first time.

"Oh, you poor things. I had such high hopes for you."

With amazing dragon speed, Dr. Dragonbreath flew around the room and devoured every single student who had broken Rule Number Five.

After being eaten by Dr. Dragonbreath, every kid in his class learned a very important life lesson about following rules and an even more important lesson about not trusting dragons that wear suits. But you'll have to read on to find out why being eaten by Dr. Dragonbreath may have actually been the best thing that could have happened to each kid.

When Dr. Dragonbreath had finished eating his class, there was only one student left alive—Cindy Chan, who had forgotten her glasses and had not been able to read Rule Number Five. She was shaking in her seat.

Dr. Dragonbreath plopped down in a chair behind his desk. "What a meal," he said, rubbing his belly. "I won't need to feed again for a year after that one."

Cindy was still frozen and shaking.

"Relax, young human. You were the only one who followed Rule Number Five, so you are perfectly safe. Now, let's not waste any more time in beginning with our lesson. Please open your notebook and take notes as I lecture on the Dragon-Human Wars of 1512."

Cindy Chan diligently took notes as she listened to Dr. Dragonbreath's fascinating lecture on the Dragon-Human Wars. His lecture was very entertaining and she learned a great deal. He was by far the best teacher Cindy had ever had. She thought it was such a shame that none of the other kids were left to learn from him, too.

Right before lunch, the classroom door opened and a new kid walked in. It was Charles Nukid.

"Hi, I'm Charles Nukid. I was in detention until just now."

"Luckily for you," said Dr. Dragonbreath, "being late for my class is *not* a rule punishable by death."

"Thank goodness," said Charles. "I'd hate to break any rule. Apparently I was out of uniform, so Nurse

Hairymoles brought me some kid named Benny Porter's clothes who didn't need them anymore. Just in time, too, 'cause Mrs. T was about to eat me."

"I didn't ask for your life story," Dr. Dragonbreath interjected. "Please be seated and read my class rules."

Charles sat down and read the first four rules to himself. Dr. Dragonbreath waited hungrily for him to read Rule Number Five, but Charles never did.

"Aren't you going to read Rule Number Five?" Dr. Dragonbreath inquired.

"Of course not! That's against the rules."

"But . . . how did you know?"

"A ghost named Derek told me as I was walking here from detention."

"I see. Derek the Ghost must like you. You're very lucky."

That afternoon, twenty-nine sets of angry parents stormed into Principal Headcrusher's office.

Randall's dad barked, "I knew his chances of survival weren't good, but on the first day? Come on!"

"Listen," said Principal Headcrusher, "if your child was eaten, it's because he or she directly disobeyed one of Dr. Dragonbreath's very simple rules. He's tough, but fair. You all signed the waiver forms. There's nothing I can do about it!"

The parents weren't satisfied and continued pressing her for answers. Finally, Principal Headcrusher said, "Look, there are billions and billions of kids in the world, but dragons are nearly extinct. The truth is, this is the secret way in which dragons are made. All of the kids Dr. Dragonbreath ate today aren't actually dead. They're just gestating in his belly, like a caterpillar inside a cocoon. In about nine months, right about when the Ghoul Games will be starting, Dr. Dragonbreath will regurgitate all of your children, and they will come out metamorphosed into young dragons."

"Wait a minute," said Randall's dad, trembling with emotion. "You're telling me that my Randall, my one and only boy, was eaten alive but isn't actually dead, and will come back in nine months changed into a dragon?"

"Yes."

". . . Cool!"

Petunia

7

Petunia's Problems

Here's the thing about Scary School: sometimes the students could be just as scary as the teachers. You might be a regular kid, but the kid sitting next to you might be a zombie, a vampire, or a werewolf. That's what made Scary School extra scary and was a big reason why Principal Headcrusher could charge so much for tuition.

Studies have shown that the more scared children are, the better they learn. After all, what could be better motivation to study than knowing your teacher will tear your arms off if you answer a question wrong? (I heard Principal Headcrusher say that in an interview last year, but more about that later.)

Principal Headcrusher wanted as many Scary kids as possible roaming around Scary School, so if you're a scary enough kid, you got to attend Scary School on a free scholarship. After all, the more Scary kids there were, the more she could charge the normal parents to send their kids there.

It was simple economics.

Petunia was one of the Scary kids who attended Scary School on a free scholarship.

As you may remember, Petunia's best friend is Frank (pronounced "Rachel"). That's why she gave her blood to save Frank's life on the first day of school. Johnny then gave Petunia his blood to save her life because he has a crush on her. The latter is a bit misleading because a lot of boys have a crush on Petunia since she is "as pretty as a petunia." Just like a petunia, she is completely purple from head to foot, she smells very nice, and her long, violet hair is covered in dusty pollen that insects collect to go make more Petunias.

Because she was so strange-looking, you might be surprised that all the boys thought Petunia was pretty, but the boys at Scary School had logical reasoning: Petunia looks just like a petunia, petunias are pretty, so Petunia must be pretty.

Petunia's biggest problem was that all the other girls in Ms. Fang's class were jealous of her beauty and weren't very nice to her at all. Most wouldn't even speak to her. The bugs constantly buzzing around her hair didn't help.

Petunia's best friend, Frank, was also her only friend. The girls weren't very nice to Frank (pronounced "Rachel") either, because of how she spelled her name, so Petunia and Frank were destined to be friends by necessity more than choice. They even signed up as a jump-rope team for the Ghoul Games together, with Petunia being Frank's jump counter.

Whenever Petunia and Frank tried to be friendly and talk to a group of girls, the girls would turn their backs and snub them. That made Petunia and Frank sad, but they were happy to at least have each other. One day when Frank was out sick, Petunia tried to sit at a lunch table with some girls from her class, but Lindsey, a prissy girl with blond pigtails, shouted, "Eww! Go away, Petunia! You have bugs flying around your hair. Bugs are gross!"

Petunia replied back as nicely as she could, "But the bugs won't bother you, I promise. They're just collecting pollen from my hair to go make more Petunias."

"I don't care what they're doing," Lindsey snorted.

"We don't want them or *you* near our food. Right, girls?"

"Yeah!" Stephanie and Maria concurred.

"Okay," said Petunia weakly, and she turned around and sat down at an empty table. As soon as she sat down, she was joined by three other Scary kids—Johnny the Sasquach, Ramon the Zombie, and Peter the Wolf. They didn't think that the bugs flying around Petunia's head were gross at all because boys like bugs. The funny thing was, Petunia was only ten years old and thought boys were gross and didn't really care for *them* buzzing around *her*. She would rather have eaten alone, but she quietly tolerated the boys' annoying antics, like belching, throwing peas at one another, and jabbering nonstop about their basketball strategies for the Ghoul Games.

Things turned bad when one of the wasps from Petunia's hair flew too close to Ramon and he swatted it away with his quick zombie reflexes. He hit it really hard, and it fell to the floor dead.

Petunia jumped up and screamed, "What did you do that for?"

Ramon was taken aback. "I'm sorry. I thought you'd be happy that I swatted one of your bugs away."

"All it wanted to do was fly away and go make more Petunias. But now it won't get to make any more Petunias because you killed it!"

"I said I'm sorry!"

Petunia tried to hold herself back from crying, but couldn't. She left her half-eaten lunch and ran out of the lunch hall, sobbing.

She continued running to the empty playground and climbed as high as she could on the monkey bars. "Stupid boys," she muttered to herself. "Stupid school."

Then she saw something in the distance. At the end of the school grounds was a twenty-foot iron gate that ensured no one could get in or out during school hours. Standing just outside the gate, looking toward her with curiosity, was another purple little girl.

Petunia stopped crying and ran as fast as she could to the end of the school grounds where the little purple girl was standing. When she got there, they both stood still and quietly stared at each other through the bars of the gate for a few moments. The girl seemed to be a couple years younger than Petunia and looked very similar. The only difference was she didn't have any bugs buzzing around her hair.

Behind the little girl was a small clearing in front of a dense, dark forest called Scary Forest. No human had ever walked through Scary Forest and come out alive on the other end.

Finally, the little girl spoke, and what she said was

the last thing Petunia expected to hear. She said, "Mommy?"

Petunia looked around. There was no one else there.

"No, I don't think so," she responded. "My name is Petunia. What's your name?"

"I'm Petunia, too! It is you, Mommy! We've been looking for you."

"What do you mean, *we*?" Petunia asked.

All of sudden, a dozen other little purple girls appeared at the edge of the forest. "Mommy!" they all shouted, and rushed toward the gate. There were little purple girls of all ages, from babies to girls nearly Petunia's age, but no one older.

"Will you come play with us?" the Little Petunias asked.

"I would," answered Petunia, "but I'm locked inside here."

"That's no problem," said Little Petunia, and all the Little Petunias made buzzing noises, and thousands of bees, wasps, and other flying insects appeared. The bugs flew right through the gate, hoisted Petunia up by her clothes, and flew her over the bars to the other side.

"Yaaay!" all the Little Petunias shouted with glee. They hugged Petunia, then grabbed her hand and began running as fast as they could into the depths of Scary Forest.

Eventually they came to a grove that was the most beautiful place Petunia had ever seen. All around were petunias of different shades and tints of violet and of all different sizes. Some were as small as regular petunias; some were as big as dinner plates; some were enormous—the size of trees! A sparkling purple river ran through the grove, and purple fish jumped in and out of the purple water.

When Petunia got there, dozens more little purple girls popped out from behind the giant petunias, and they all cried with joy and hugged their "Mommy." Petunia had never felt so loved, so accepted, or so popular in her entire life.

"Tell us a story, Mommy!" they insisted.

"Okay," said Petunia. And all afternoon Petunia told the Little Petunias stories from the many books she had read. The girls brought Petunia delicious purple berries to eat and refreshing purple water to drink, and Petunia even got to see a brand-new purple baby pop out of the ground.

"So all those bugs really do fly off to make more Petunias!" said Petunia, laughing.

"Of course!" said the first Little Petunia. "You're the Petunia Queen. You're the only one who can make more Little Petunias. That's why you're our mommy."

"Well," said Petunia, "it has been really nice meeting all of you, but I have to get back to school now."

"You're leaving us, Mommy? But why?" asked Little Petunia.

"Because," she said, "I have a mommy, too, who is supposed to pick me up after school and is probably worried sick about me. But I promise I'll come back to visit real soon."

Petunia began to walk out of the petunia grove, and all the Little Petunias started crying.

Geez, she thought. Grow up.

Petunia continued walking, but when she got to the edge of the grove, an enormous petunia dropped in front of her and blocked her way out. She tried to run around it, but then more giant petunias dropped down all around the perimeter of the grove, trapping her hopelessly inside.

"You are our mommy," stated the first Little Petunia. "You can't leave."

"But I don't want to be a mommy," said Petunia. "It's not fair!"

"Life isn't all purple berries," said Little Petunia, with none of the joy she'd had before. "Don't you understand you have to stay with us forever?" Then her giggling smile came back and she said, "Now please tell us another story!"

And all the Little Petunias chanted, "New story! New story! New story!" They pulled Petunia onto a bed of petunias and jumped up with her.

Petunia started weeping, thinking she would never see her parents or any of her classmates again, but the Little Petunias didn't care. She realized at that moment that being the most popular person wasn't for her at all. Petunia just wanted to be back in Scary School where all the girls hated her.

The Little Petunias kept poking her, so she started a new story. "Once upon a ti—"

Boom! One of the giant petunias exploded in a huge ball of smoke and fire. From behind the smoke, a whole legion of Scary School teachers emerged, including Principal Headcrusher, Ms. Fang, Nurse Hairymoles, and Mr. Spider-Eyes.

The Little Petunias screamed and started running, but they couldn't go far because the giant wall of petunias kept them in. Nurse Hairymoles dragged in the big fire hose (which had been extended after the Mr. Acidbath incident) and started spraying all the Little Petunias with clear water. When each one of them got wet, their legs turned into stems, their hands turned into leaves, and their heads and hair turned into purple petals and pistils.

Soon, all the Little Petunias had turned into regular little petunias sprouting from the ground.

Petunia ran to Principal Headcrusher, who hugged her (very delicately) with her strong, oversized hands.

"How did you know where I was?" Petunia asked.

"This is a very good school, Petunia. You don't think we have security cameras?" Principal Headcrusher replied.

Then Petunia's parents showed up, and Petunia hugged them harder than she ever had before.

"Thank you for finding our daughter," Petunia's parents said to Principal Headcrusher.

"Of course! You didn't think we would let anything bad happen to one of our scariest kids, did you?"

On the way home, Petunia stopped at a barber shop and had them cut her hair very short. She wore a hat the rest of the year.

Whenever a bug flew near her, she swatted it dead.

8

The
Golden Torch

At 8:03 a.m. on October 1, Principal Head-crusher's voice sounded through the PA system of Scary School. "I have just received a surprise visit from the gracious chairman of the Ghoul Games, Mr. Franz Dietrich Wolfbark. He has informed me that the traditional running of the Ghoul Games torch will begin this afternoon at the front entrance of the school. Following lunch, everyone is to gather at Scary Fountain, where one lucky student will carry the torch and hand it to the one and only Frankenstein. Frankenstein will start the torch's

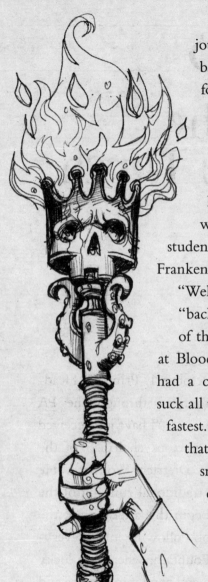

journey all around the world before it arrives back here for the start of the Ghoul Games this spring. That is all."

After the loudspeaker crackled off, Wendy raised her hand. "Ms. Fang, how will they choose which student gets to pass the torch to Frankenstein?"

"Well," replied Ms. Fang, "back when I was a young girl of three hundred sixteen years at Bloodington Elementary, they had a contest to see who could suck all the blood out of a troll the fastest. But I doubt they will do that with you. The troll would smash you before you could get close enough. It wouldn't even be fair."

All the students gulped.

After lunch, everyone ran to Scary Fountain

at the front entrance of the school. They still didn't know who would be the one to hand off the torch to Frankenstein.

There was so much excitement, even Archie the giant squid raised his ten-foot eyeball out of the murky moat to witness the event.

"Look!" shouted Mr. Spider-Eyes, pointing to the sky.

High in the air, Franz Dietrich Wolfbark was riding on the back of a ferocious-looking gargoyle. He held up a golden, unlit torch. From across the street atop Goblin Hill, a goblin band was trying to play a song of triumph for him, but their instruments were completely out of tune and none of them played very well. Everyone covered their ears and tried to imagine something much better playing.

The gargoyle landed and Mr. Wolfbark hopped off. The students recoiled at his sunken, skeletal face and drab gray suit; but then he held up the Golden Torch, and as it shimmered in the sunlight, the crowd cheered and whistled. The gargoyle stepped in front of Wolfbark and bowed, basking in the applause. Mr. Wolfbark hit the gargoyle on the head with the Golden Torch.

"Ouchers!" yelped the gargoyle.

"Stop hogging the spotlight, filthy gargoyle!" Mr. Wolfbark barked. "Fly back to your perch."

Frank
N.
Stein

The gargoyle slumped over and muttered, "I hate my life." Then he flew back to his perch atop Petrified Pavilion.

"Good afternoon, students of Scary School. I am Franz Dietrich Wolfbark, the chairman of this year's Ghoul Games."

Mr. Wolfbark paused as if expecting more applause, but nobody clapped because they were sick of doing it by that point.

Wolfbark continued, "Yes, well, to explain how this works, once the Golden Torch is lit, one lucky student will carry it across the yard to our very special guest . . . the one . . . the only . . . Frank N. Stein!"

At that moment, a donut-shaped car sputtered its way down the street and pulled onto the side curb. The door opened, and a short man in a button-down shirt and high-waisted trousers stepped out. It was the closest thing he had in his closet to a jogging suit. He was pudgy and middle-aged, with thick glasses and a balding head of frizzy brown hair.

"Hello, children!" the man said. "My name is Frank N. Stein. I own Frank N. Stein's Donut Shop on the other side of town. You've probably never seen it. It's in a terrible location next to an abandoned gas station."

The students were all getting anxious and starting to grumble.

"Hey!" exclaimed Ramon. "Where's Frankenstein? I thought we were going to see the Frankenstein monster!"

"Such a smart kid!" proclaimed Frank N. Stein. "But if you'd actually read the book *Frankenstein* by Mary Shelley, you would know that Frankenstein is not the name of the monster, it's the name of the monster's creator, Dr. Frankenstein. The monster is referred to simply as 'the monster.' Mary Shelley was not good with names."

"Aaaaw phooey!" all the kids groaned in frustration, realizing they weren't going to get to see the real Frankenstein monster.

"But," continued Frank N. Stein, "the good news is that the original Dr. Frankenstein was in fact a distant relative of mine. He left me the secret instructions on how to make a patented Frankenstein monster, so I spent last weekend digging up graves, sewing together old body parts, and bringing an abomination of nature to life. And what do you know, it worked! I made a patented Frankenstein monster just for *you*! I named it Murray."

All the kids cheered, "Yaaaaay! Where is it?"

"Where is it? What a great question! Who knows? As soon as it came to life, it kicked me in the groin and ran off. I'm pretty sure it's been trudging through nearby villages wreaking havoc."

Mr. Wolfbark stepped in. "Isn't he great, folks? Now, normally we would have each student fight a troll to the death to determine who would carry the torch to the amazing Frank N. Stein over here, but unfortunately you humans are too weak for it to be a fair fight, so instead we chose the student with the highest grades. That student is . . ."

From atop Goblin Hill, a goblin played a drum roll.

"Cindy Chan. Congratulations."

Everyone was silent except for one burst of clapping and cheering from Charles Nukid. Nobody else in the school knew who Cindy Chan was. Aside from Charles, all the other kids in her class had been eaten by Dr. Dragonbreath, and she never dared even look at anyone else in the school for fear of breaking Dr. Dragonbreath's Rule Number Three.

Cindy Chan managed a slight smile as she stepped forward and was handed the Golden Torch by Mr. Wolfbark.

"Hold the torch skyward, Cindy," whispered Wolfbark.

As she did so, Dr. Dragonbreath swooped over the crowd and blew a jet of fire across the yard, officially lighting the Golden Torch.

Everyone cheered.

"Now Cindy," whispered Wolfbark, "bring the torch over to Frank N. Stein so we can get this over with."

"Yes, sir," said Cindy. "I'll twy my best." Cindy carefully began walking, making sure she didn't ruin the moment by tripping and dropping the torch.

That was when the ground started shaking. In the distance, a rumbling was heard that became louder and louder. Everyone was getting scared and looking around nervously. Soon, the great rumbling seemed right on top of them, and the cause of the rumbling was revealed. . . .

It was a mob of people. They were carrying torches, raising pitchforks, screaming, "Kill the monster! Kill the monster!"

Ahead of the mob, Frank N. Stein's monster was running for its life, trying its best to move quickly despite having legs of different sizes, a torso that was rotted away, and arms it had no control over. They were flailing about and continuously hitting the monster in the face.

Cindy was just thirty feet away from Frank N. Stein when the monster charged past her, holding something to its ear, followed closely by the angry mob still chanting, "Kill the monster!"

Frank N. Stein stepped in front of the mob, bringing everyone to halt.

"Stop this!" demanded Frank N. Stein. "This is *my* monster. I made it. What's all this fuss about?"

"It's hideous!" shouted a villager.

"Okay, okay, it's not as pretty as a jelly donut, but is being ugly such a crime?"

"Yes!" shouted Lindsey from the crowd of students.

"Feh! Then I should have been locked up ages ago!" replied Frank N. Stein, to waves of laughter.

Another villager piped up, "It somehow got ahold of a cell phone and goes into our movie

theaters and talks straight through every movie!"

"Is that true, Murray?" asked Frank N. Stein.

The monster did not respond because it was busy talking on its cell phone.

"Okay," said Frank N. Stein, "that's just plain rude. Go ahead and kill it. I'll make one with better manners next time."

Frank N. Stein stepped out of the way, and the chase was back on. The monster ran for its life (while still talking on the phone) as the angry villagers followed behind.

Unfortunately, one of the villagers who didn't have a torch grabbed the Golden Torch out of Cindy's hand as they ran by. With all the commotion, nobody noticed the Golden Torch was missing from Cindy's hand until the mob was far in the distance.

"Where did the Golden Torch go?" exclaimed a furious Mr. Wolfbark.

"One . . . one . . . one of the viwagers took it," squeaked Cindy. "I'm vewy, vewy sowwy."

"Well, that's just *great*," said Wolfbark. "Why do I even try to do anything nice for you humans when you consistently mess everything up? That's it. There will be no torch running this year."

"Aaaaw," moaned the crowd.

"Don't *aaaaw* me! I have no human feelings of pity. This event is over! Useless humans, this is probably the last time you'll see me before the start of the Ghoul Games this spring. The monsters all over the world are going to be terribly upset that they didn't get to run with the Golden Torch and will no doubt take out their anger on all of you during the Ghoul Games. So remember, no matter how much you practice, you stand no chance of beating the monsters from the other schools and you will be eaten as soon as you lose. I advise you to make the most of your final days."

Jerry the gargoyle flew over to Mr. Wolfbark, who climbed on top of his back. They lifted off into the sky without even saying good-bye.

Frank N. Stein was still standing there, looking quite saddened. "Welp, I guess I trained all year for nothing. I suppose I'll go home and feed my cat. If she doesn't get fed by four o'clock she pees everywhere. Here, take these flyers for my donut shop and drop in sometime."

Every student took a flyer that read, "FRANK N. STEIN'S DONUT SHOP: CHEWY, DELICIOUS DONUTS AND HORRIBLE ABOMINATIONS OF NATURE MADE FRESH DAILY."

As Mr. Wolfbark flew off on the gargoyle, and Frank N. Stein's donut car sputtered away, and the kids walked back to class, the goblin band played a terrible song that sounded like a herd of elephants drowning in a tar pit.

Frank (*not* Frank N. Stein, but the Frank that is pronounced "Rachel") said to Petunia, "Maybe it wouldn't be so bad to get eaten by a monster at the Ghoul Games so I wouldn't have to see scenes like this ever again."

9

The Terrifying
Mr. Turtlesnaps

First off, let's make something clear: his name is pronounced "Mr. Turtle-Snaps" *not* "Mr. Turtles-Naps." Second, he's not a turtle, he's a giant land tortoise, and don't you forget it. There's a huge difference. For one, unlike turtles, tortoises live entirely above water, only wading into streams to clean themselves or to drink. In fact, they could drown in a deep or swift current. Turtles love the water.

On a spring morning last year, Mr. Turtlesnaps had an interview with Principal Headcrusher to become a teacher at Scary School.

Mr.
Turtlesnaps

He showed up fifteen minutes late and crawled slowly into the principal's office. With great effort, he hoisted himself up on his hind legs and plopped down in a chair.

"You're late," said Principal Headcrusher.

Mr. Turtlesnaps answered in a soft voice that evoked ancient wisdom. "Sorry, but you try being on time when your top speed is one mile per hour on a slick surface."

"Normally, I would crush a teacher's head for being so late," warned Principal Headcrusher, raising her hands and making a crushing gesture with her enormous fists.

"I'll keep that in mind," Mr. Turtlesnaps replied.

"What brings you to Scary School, Mr. Turtlesnaps?"

"I got fired from Animal School."

"What for?"

"Being late too much."

"And why won't that happen if you work here?"

"Scary School is much closer to my home. I live right across the street."

"Across the street? But there are no houses across the street."

"I know. I live on top of Goblin Hill and spend most of my time lying on a flat rock that gets nice and hot. Me oh my, I do love that rock."

"I suppose that makes sense. But to the point: you may have heard that our science teacher, Mr. Acidbath, suffered a terrible Fear Gas accident during one of his classes and will be recovering from that mishap for the better part of his life. We're looking for someone to fill in for him for the next fifty years or so."

"Sounds tuuuurtle-iffic," said Mr. Turtlesnaps, chuckling to himself.

Principal Headcrusher didn't get the joke and went on. "Just what makes you qualified to teach science?" she probed.

"I lived on the Galápagos Islands nearly all of my life. Back when I was a young tortoise of seventy-five, a scientist named Darwin came and lived with us for a spell. We became friends and when he passed on, he left me all his books on science. I'm a bit of a slow reader, but I spent the next sixty years reading all the books, and when I finished reading one, I immediately ate the book to make sure I had fully digested the material."

"Impressive. Well, I have no doubts about your scientific expertise, but I'm not sure you would fit in at this school."

"Why not?"

"I think you're perfectly suited for Animal School,

but I just don't see what could possibly be scary about a turtle."

"Tortoise," he interjected. "And don't you forget it."

"Whatever you are, you seem to be kind, slow, and quite adorable in an odd sort of way."

"You're saying I need to be scarier in order to teach here?"

"Yes. Studies have shown that the more scared children are, the better they learn. After all, what could be better motivation to study than knowing your teacher will tear your arms off if you answer a question wrong? Parents pay good money for their children to come here and be scared out of their wits at all times. If every so often we lose one of our students, well, as your friend must have taught you, it's survival of the fittest."

"He didn't teach me that. I taught him."

"Be that as it may, I just don't see you *fitting in* here," said Principal Headcrusher, chuckling to herself.

"Hmm . . ." Mr. Turtlesnaps lowered his head and scratched his noggin with his stumpy foot, then suddenly he sprang up and yelled, "Boo!"

Principal Headcrusher didn't flinch one bit.

"Okay, I guess you're right," muttered Mr. Turtlesnaps, and he quickly drew his arms and legs inside his shell and plopped down onto the floor with a thud. Then he popped his arms and legs back out and slowly crawled toward the door.

But before he got there, he stopped, seemed to think of something, and slowly curled his head around like a question mark toward Principal Headcrusher.

"Tell me something," he said. "Do you think millions of folks dying is scary?"

"Yes, of course," replied Principal Headcrusher.

"What about tiny, invisible organisms that eat you alive from the inside?"

"That's very scary, too."

"What about all the fish and beautiful creatures in the sea suddenly disappearing?"

"Stop it. You really are starting to scare me now."

"Well, well." Mr. Turtlesnaps smiled. "All I'm telling you are facts of science. Science shows us that climate change is causing the polar ice caps to melt, which will lead to millions of folks dying in floods, hurricanes, and droughts. Science also shows us that all the tiny bacteria and viruses are growing stronger and evolving faster than we can come up with cures, and all the toxic sewage we're dumping into the ocean is destroying coral reefs and all the other sea life we love so much. So just because I'm not scary myself, that doesn't mean the class I teach won't be scary."

Principal Headcrusher was speechless.

Mr. Turtlesnaps turned his head around and

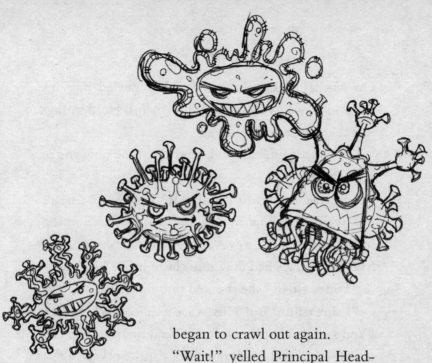

began to crawl out again.

"Wait!" yelled Principal Head-crusher. "I hope I don't regret this, but . . . you're hired."

"Well, thank you," he said. "I have always believed that the changes happening in the world are what kids should be afraid of, not all these vampires, werewolves, and other creepies running around."

"Just one word of warning," said Principal Head-crusher as she opened the door for him. "Nothing irks me more than tardiness. If you are late for just one of your classes, I will squish your head like a grape, and then I will *fire you*!"

"Agreed," said Mr. Turtlesnaps with a smile.

On Mr. Turtlesnaps's first day, he crawled into his classroom twenty minutes late. Principal Headcrusher was there waiting for him.

"I warned you," she said, seething, "and now you're going to get it!"

She reached out to squish Mr. Turtlesnaps's head, but when she opened her fist, there was nothing inside. Usually there was a gooey mess. She realized Mr. Turtlesnaps had drawn his head inside his shell.

"You're fired!" she shouted into his shell.

"I don't think so!" his voice echoed back to her. "You said you had to crush my head first and *then* fire me. So until you crush my head, I still work here!"

"I suppose you're right. You got very lucky."

"Would you call it luck that I've lived to be two hundred and fifty years old with maniacs like *you* running around? It's survival of the fittest, my lady. Survival of the fittest!"

10

The Best
Lunch Ever

You probably think lunch at Scary School is a grotesque buffet of gross stuff like worms and maggots and gruel and guts.

If that's what you think, then you are *wrong*. In fact, you couldn't be more wrong.

Lunch at Scary School is *amazing*. I mean, it's ridiculously good. Can you guess why? Okay, go ahead, I'll read your mind. . . .

Nope. That's not it. I'll just tell you, or we could be here all day. The reason is because every lunch a student eats at Scary School may very well be his or her last meal. Imagine what you would choose if you could eat anything in the world for your last meal—that's how good lunch is at Scary School.

There is no lunch bell. Everyday at noon sharp, Mrs. T, the T. rex in a blue dress, gets hungry and she lets out an earthshaking roar, causing everyone for miles to cover their ears. At that point, she either eats whatever kid is still stuck in detention, or she goes on a hunt in Scary Forest, but more about that later.

A couple months into the school year, autumn had slowly crept into the surroundings. The trees had turned deep shades of orange and red, reminding

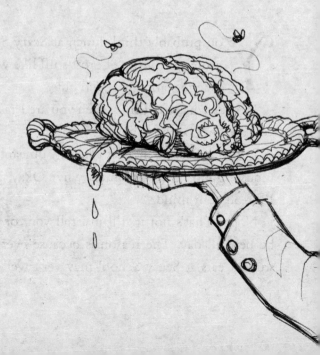

everyone that Halloween was fast approaching. On this day, right after Mrs. T's lunch roar, all the classes lined up together at the lunch hall and waited to be seated by the zombie waiters. The newly renovated lunch hall had just reopened and it looked like the inside of the fanciest restaurant you've ever seen.

The ceiling was at least thirty feet tall, with enormous candlelit chandeliers hanging down over each class's table. To promote school unity for the Ghoul Games, every class now sat together at their own

big table. Every grade, third through sixth, had two classes of thirty kids to start off the year, so in total there were eight round tables, which seated thirty kids each.

Ms. Fang's table was the only one that had each seat occupied. Every other table had at least two or three empty chairs due to students who had made an early exit from their state of being. Dr. Dragonbreath's table had only poor Charles Nukid and Cindy Chan, sitting all by themselves.

Once everyone was seated, the zombie waiters handed every kid their own menu.

"For today's special," moaned the zombie waiters, "we highly recommend the brains. The brraaaaaainnnnns!" Sure enough, on the menu was a dish called shark-brains ravioli with sage and lemon. Most of the boys ordered that. The three Rachels ordered the steamed wild salmon with chili oil, ginger, baby bok choy, snap peas, and jasmine rice. Lindsey ordered the roast Maine lobster with potato purée, chanterelles, edamame, and tarragon. Benny Porter, the vampire kid, ordered the blood sausage with apples and baby squash.

The zombie waiters lurched into the kitchen and handed all the orders to the chef. The chef only had twenty minutes to prepare every meal for the hundreds of kids so they would have enough time to eat, play, and be back to class in an hour. Plus, the chef made everything to order so it would be at its freshest. Nothing was ever cold or stale. How was the chef able to accomplish this, you ask? Because the chef was a giant octopus named Sue.

At the end of each of Sue's eight long arms was either a pot, a pan, a spatula, a mixer, a knife, a bowl, a measuring spoon, or a strainer. What made it all the more amazing was that she did all her cooking from inside a giant water tank with holes punched in the walls for her arms to fit through. Plus, there were wheels on the bottom of her tank so that she could move around wherever she needed to go.

The kids called her Sue the Amazing Octo-Chef. She had trained with the world's scariest and best chefs, including WereWolfgang Puck, Mario Bat-Ali, and Scary Danko. Her philosophy was, "Fresh food makes for fresh minds." All the fruits and vegetables she cooked with were grown right down the hill on the Scary School Farm. All the fish were caught fresh in nearby Gremlin River, and the meat was freshly hunted and caught by Scary School teachers. Everything was local, seasonal, and delicious.

At home, most of the kids wouldn't touch the vegetables on their plates, but at Scary School, the veggies

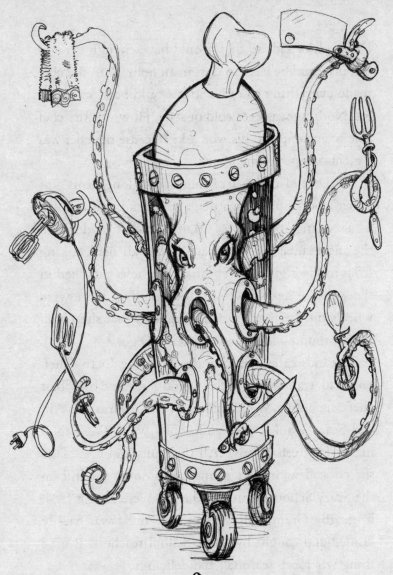

Sue
the Amazing
Octo-Chef

were so perfectly cooked that the kids gobbled up greens like they were candy. When the shark-brains ravioli came out, the boys were a bit disappointed that it didn't taste stranger. The brains were very soft and mild-tasting; it was like eating marshmallow mushrooms. But the best part of lunch was dessert.

On this day, when everyone had cleared their plates and eaten all their vegetables, the zombies dragged out the biggest pumpkin anyone had ever seen. It was so big, you could probably fit every kid from Ms. Fang's class inside it. The hall erupted with cheers when they saw it.

Sue the Amazing Octo-Chef wheeled herself out into the dining area. She held a microphone up to the tank and said, "Fall marks the start of pumpkin season, so using some special Scary School magic, we've grown the biggest pumpkin in history! I'm sure you are all familiar with the idea of catching your dinner, but have you ever had to catch your dessert?"

Everyone shook their heads and looked at one another with excitement.

"Well then," continued Sue, "this is your chance. Jason, will you please do the honors."

Jason climbed to the very top of the pumpkin. Using his chainsaw, he cut a big hole at the top, and he tugged on the stem with all his might until it popped

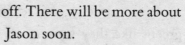

off. There will be more about Jason soon.

All of sudden, hundreds of jack-o'-lanterns hopped out of the giant pumpkin and started bouncing all over the room.

"Catch a pumpkin to catch your dessert!" Sue exclaimed.

Every kid at Scary School jumped out of their seat and started running to try to catch the bouncing pumpkins. They were bounding all over the room like crazy balls, laughing through their jack-o'-lantern grins. The pumpkins were covered in pumpkin slime that made them very slippery and tough to hold on to. Whenever a kid grabbed one, it slipped right through their hands a second later.

"Come on!" exclaimed Sue. "Your strength and agility won't help you in the Ghoul Games against all the monsters you'll be facing. You're going to have to learn to use your brains in order to win!"

For nearly the rest of lunchtime, nobody could figure out how to catch any of the pumpkins. They were just too slippery. Then, Charles Nukid had an idea.

He went back to his seat at the big empty table and sat down. Soon, a bouncing pumpkin landed right in his lap. He didn't try to touch it or grab it. He just looked at the pumpkin, and the pumpkin looked back at him as he patted his head to make sure no hairs were out of place.

"Aren't you going to try to catch me?" asked the pumpkin.

"No," said Charles. "I know that *your* whole purpose in life is to be eaten, and *I* want to eat you for my nourishment. So, since we're helping each other out, the least I can do is let you choose when you want to be eaten."

"Thank you," said the pumpkin. "I think now is a good time."

The pumpkin popped off its top for Charles, and inside was a smooth, creamy pumpkin custard. Charles started eating the custard and he thought it was the best thing he had ever tasted.

Soon, everyone noticed that Charles was eating his pumpkin and said, "Look! The new kid caught a pumpkin! How did you do it?"

Charles told everyone how to catch a pumpkin, and the kids ran back to their seats and let the pumpkins come to them. Soon they were all enjoying their delicious pumpkin custard, and Charles became the new school hero.

After that lunch, everyone called him Charles instead of "new kid." Charles thought it was weird that everyone suddenly started calling him by his first name instead of his last name, but he was happy to be called *any* name other than Toothpick.

11
Monster
Math

An hour after lunch, Ms. Fang said to her class, "I have a special surprise for you today."

No one clapped because kids didn't like surprises at Scary School. For instance, back when I was still alive, my friend Tim and I decided to eat lunch outside on a beautiful day. We sat down on a bench, but then a Petrified Pavilion gargoyle swooped down and snatched Tim's roast beef sandwich right out of his hands. Tim chased the gargoyle trying to get it back, but he got too close to Petrified Pavilion and was snatched up by another gargoyle and became a roast beef lunch himself.

Tim was very surprised he had become a gargoyle's lunch. The gargoyles were surprised to be having such a great meal. I wasn't surprised at all because Tim was not very smart. But back to Ms. Fang's class.

"Are you ready for your surprise, class?" Ms. Fang asked.

Everyone leaned back and shook their heads.

"Too bad. Here it is!"

Into the room walked the weirdest monster the class had ever seen. It was big and round, covered in pink fur, and had giant lobster claws. It had the head of a lion and the tail of a stingray. It also had a very cute, sparkly purse that Lindsey, Stephanie, and Maria noticed and liked.

"Class, this is Ms. Stingbottom. In honor of the Ghoul Games, there is a teacher exchange program, and she will be visiting here every Friday to teach you Monster Math."

"Hellooooo," Ms. Stingbottom said. Her voice had a silly, singsong quality. "I am soooo excited to be teaching human children the wonders of my species's unique mathematical system. Awoo-Aloo!"

The class stared with blank faces.

"*Awoo-Aloo*," Ms. Fang explained, "is a monster phrase that establishes trust. When a monster says it, you have to say it back exactly the same way, or it is a major insult and you'll have to do battle."

"Awoo-Aloo!" the class proclaimed. Ms. Stingbottom was so happy, she did a full backflip.

"My name is Ms. Stingbottom, *not Stink*bottom, and if I hear any of you call me *Stink*bottom, you can say good-bye to both your arms," warned Ms. Stingbottom, snapping her lobster pincers. "And with no way to wipe your bottom, *then* we'll see who the real *Stink*bottom is, won't we?"

The class laughed. That made Ms. Stingbottom happy, and she did another backflip.

Ms. Stingbottom continued, "Now that we have the serious stuff out of the way, let's have fun and do some Monster Math!"

The class groaned. No one except Johnny liked doing math.

"I know, I know," said Ms. Stingbottom. "Math is boooring. But I think you'll see that Monster Math is quite different. I'll need a volunteer for the first problem."

Johnny was the only one who raised his hand, and Ms. Stingbottom called him up to the front of the room. In case you don't remember Johnny, he has a crush on Petunia, his friends are Ramon and Peter, and he has messy, light brown hair and one big freckle

1+1=1,0

Ms. Stingbottom

on the tip of his nose. He's also a young Sasquatch, and hoped to become a Bigfoot, once his feet grew bigger.

"What's your name, young man?"

"Johnny," said Johnny.

"Okay, Johnny. What is five plus three?"

"Eight," said Johnny, without a moment's hesitation. The class applauded.

"Aaaahh!" shrieked Ms. Stingbottom. "Don't you ever say that number to me again! Oh my goodness gracious. And how dare you all applaud him! He is *wrong*."

The class gasped. Johnny had never gotten a math question wrong before.

"No, I'm not," he said. "Look."

Johnny held up five fingers on one hand and three on the other and counted them, one through eight.

"I don't care what your fingers tell

you," said Ms. Stingbottom. "Are you saying your fingers are smarter than *me*?"

"No, I just—"

"I say that five plus three equals nine hundred fifty-six," said Ms. Stingbottom matter-of-factly. "What do you think of that?"

"I don't think that's right," said Johnny.

"Well, I'm a big, scary monster, and I say that five plus three equals nine hundred fifty-six, and unless you tell me I'm right, I'm going to cut your nose off."

"No! Not my nose!" pleaded Johnny. "It has my freckle on it!"

"Well then, what does five plus three equal?" asked Ms. Stingbottom, holding her pincer to Johnny's nose.

Johnny gave in and reluctantly said, "Nine hundred fifty-six."

"Very good!" proclaimed Ms. Stingbottom. "You just learned how to do Monster Math. You may have a seat."

Johnny walked back to his desk, feeling defeated, as Ms. Stingbottom continued, "You see, there are a couple very simple principles to follow that can make anyone an expert at Monster Math. First: Monsters *love* big numbers. We *hate* small numbers. They actually scare us, as you saw before when Johnny said that dreadful little number. Second: When you're doing

Monster Math with a monster, the monster is always right. If you tell us a really big number, we will usually want an even bigger one, 'cause the bigger the number, the happier we become. Let's try another problem, shall we?"

Next, Lindsey went up to the front of the room.

"What's six plus nine?" Ms. Stingbottom asked.

"Six thousand eighty-two!" said Lindsey with glee.

"Oooh. Very close," said Ms. Stingbottom, "but the correct answer is six thousand two hundred forty-four."

"Of course; six thousand two hundred forty-four. You're right," said Lindsey.

That made Ms. Stingbottom extra happy, and she did a double backflip.

Next, Jason rushed up to the front of the room.

"Oh my, what a wonderfully scary-looking boy you are," said Ms. Stingbottom, admiring Jason's distorted face, which had suffered a few too many hockey pucks to the nose and jaw. "Here's a tough one. What's twenty minus seven?"

"Twelve million, five hundred thousand!" said Jason.

"That's exactly right!" said Ms. Stingbottom. "I couldn't have done better myself." Then she bent way down and did a triple backflip, she was so happy.

"Awooooo-Alooooo!" she proclaimed.

"Awooooo-Alooooo!" the class happily shouted back.

"I think we have time for just one more," said Ms. Stingbottom.

Wendy Crumkin, the smart girl with freckles, stepped to the front of the room.

"This is a tricky one," said Ms. Stingbottom. "Pay close attention. What's zero times zero?"

"Infinity," said Wendy.

Ms. Stingbottom fainted.

12

A Horrible Halloween

At regular schools, Halloween is the one day every year when everyone and everything is allowed to be scary.

At Scary School it's the exact opposite. Because it's *always* scary at Scary School, Halloween is the one day when absolutely *nothing* is scary.

Every teacher is as sweet as can be and isn't allowed to tear off limbs, maim, or eat any of the kids. Dr. Dragonbreath even takes down his rules, and so Charles Nukid and Cindy Chan looked at each other for the first time during class. The gargoyles went on vacation, the Venus flytraps went to sleep, and Mrs. T put corks on her teeth.

This year on Halloween, Principal Headcrusher decided that every student should come to school dressed up in a Halloween costume for a costume contest. The winner's prize would be a dragon-back ride with Dr. Dragonbreath as he flew above Goblin Hill on his daily patrol.

Every kid was scared to death of winning the costume contest. They were sure Dr. Dragonbreath would eat them during the ride, so nobody wore a costume on Halloween. The only two who came dressed up were Fred and Charles Nukid. Fred came dressed up as a dragon hunter. The kids were now certain that Fred had a death wish.

Charles Nukid came dressed as Dr. Dragonbreath's Rule Number Five. He was sure he would have the scariest costume and was really hoping to win. Charles Nukid liked Dr. Dragonbreath because he was the only thing, man or beast, who liked rules as much as he did.

During Ms. Fang's class, the kids were relishing their one day of guaranteed safety.

Jason took out his chainsaw and sawed everyone's desks into kid-sized hockey sticks. The class played a game of hockey while Ms. Fang was trying to teach a lesson on fractions. At first she was furious that she couldn't suck the blood of the students causing the commotion, but soon she realized that her lesson in fractions had been put to practical use since Jason had cut all the desks into perfectly proportioned hockey sticks. Satisfied with her remarkable teaching, Ms. Fang sat back at her desk and cheered the classroom hockey game.

At one point, Johnny stole Petunia's hat and played keep-away with it. By stealing her hat, Johnny was trying to show Petunia that he liked her, but Petunia didn't get it and got very angry. A hive of bees had been waiting

patiently for Petunia's hat to come off and swarmed the classroom. Johnny finally gave her hat back after everyone had gotten stung.

During lunch, Principal Headcrusher walked into the lunch hall to tell everyone to report to Petrified Pavilion for the results of the costume contest. To her surprise, the lunch hall was empty. All the kids were already at Petrified Pavilion, enjoying the freedom of sneaking inside without being eaten by a gargoyle.

Principal Headcrusher made her way up to Petrified Pavilion, stood on the stage and put her enormous hands to her mouth, which amplified her voice ten times louder than any microphone could. The kids in the front row would suffer minor to significant hearing loss.

"Before we get to the costume contest," Principal Headcrusher proclaimed, "I have a very special surprise."

Everyone groaned.

"The goblins that live on Goblin Hill have come all the way from across the street to perform a Halloween play for you. They've been working very hard on it for almost two days, so I expect you to give them your full attention."

Curtains opened, and a gaggle of at least fifty goblins stormed the stage. They were very small, about two feet tall, with long pointy ears, sharp claws, and teeth that weren't very scary, and big poufs of colorful hair. Some of the goblins were doing a strange dance, but some of them weren't. They seemed pretty disorganized.

One of the goblins was wearing a red suit and had a big pouf of red hair. He stepped forward and said in a voice that was high and gravelly, as if he had just inhaled helium, "Good afternoon. I am your narrator. The goblins of Goblin Hill are pleased to present the famous tale of *The Three Little Pigs!*"

All the kids clapped because they liked this story.

The goblins cleared the stage in a mad dash so that the narrator was left alone to commence the action.

"Once upon a time," said the goblin narrator in the red suit, "there were three little pigs."

Three goblins crawled onto the stage wearing pig costumes with snouts and curly tails. The kids laughed and cheered.

The narrator continued. "Each little pig held an advanced degree in architecture, so each decided to build his own house."

A group of goblins wearing yellow straw outfits rushed onto the stage and jumped on top of each others' shoulders with amazing gymnastic ability. Working together, they formed the shape of a house around the first little pig, complete with chimneys, windows, and doors.

"The first little pig missed the day in class when they taught them *not* to build houses out of straw. So, he built his house out of *grade C* straw—the cheapest, flimsiest straw on the market. He was not a smart pig.

"The second little pig was a little bit smarter. He built his house out of twigs. Still not very smart, but definitely better than grade C straw."

Three Little Pigs

Another group of goblins wearing brown twig costumes rushed the stage and formed a twig house.

"The third little pig was the smartest. He built his house out of bricks." And more goblins wearing red brick costumes jumped on each other's shoulders and formed a brick house.

The narrator whispered in a scary tone, "Then, one day, a hungry wolf came into town."

A goblin wearing a very strange wolf costume walked onto the stage, growling. It looked like the goblin actor had glued blades of grass all over himself to resemble fur.

The narrator continued, "The wolf slunk to the house made of straw. When the little pig refused to let him in, the wolf huffed, and puffed, and blew his house down!"

A goblin stagehand turned on a gigantic electric fan, and a huge gust of wind hit the straw house of goblins. They all fell over on top of one another and crushed the poor pig goblin inside. The goblins were moaning and groaning and seemed to be in a great deal of pain.

The kids in the audience looked around for some acknowledgment that it was part of the show, but everyone seemed equally confused.

"Ha-ha-ha!" laughed the narrator. "The wolf

feasted on the stupid pig that built his house of straw."

The wolf goblin started doing a dance of joy, apparently to distract the audience from looking at the injured goblins being pulled off the stage. It wasn't working.

"Next, the wolf went to the house that was made of twigs. The pig refused to let him in, so the wolf huffed and puffed and blew *that* pig's house down!"

The gigantic fan was turned up even higher this time, and all the goblins that formed the twig house went flying across Petrified Pavilion like they had been shot out of cannons. They hit the back wall and slid down to the floor. They moaned and groaned in their high-pitched, gravelly voices, "That hurt!" "Not good!" "Ouchie-wouchies!"

The kids in the audience were even more horrified. Many started crying and wanted to leave, but remained seated for the sheer morbid curiosity of what would happen next.

"Ha-ha-ha!" laughed the narrator once again. "The wolf enjoyed his second course of stupid pig even more than the first one."

The wolf goblin finished another silly dance while the injured goblins were quickly carried out of sight, and then he approached the house of brick.

The narrator spoke softly to build the tension:

"Finally, the wolf came to the smart pig's house made out of bricks. No matter how hard he huffed and puffed, he couldn't blow the house down. *So . . .* the wolf called his brothers, who were in the demolition business. They brought in a crane and a wrecking ball and aimed it at the brick house."

Suddenly, a giant wrecking ball dropped from the ceiling of Petrified Pavilion. The stagehand goblins gave the wrecking ball a big push, and it began swinging across the stage.

"Look out!" the children in the audience shouted, but the brick-house goblins held their position and were hit by the enormous wrecking ball. They went flying all over the place. Some goblins weren't hit at first and remained onstage, exhaling a big sigh of relief, but then the wrecking ball swung back toward them and they got clunked and went flying in the other direction, screaming, "Aaaaaaaagh!"

The narrator finished the story by saying, "And so all the pigs were eaten by the wolf, as is the correct nature of the food chain. Even the smartest pig on Earth is no match for a hungry wolf who has connections in the demolition business. The En—"

The narrator goblin's final word was cut off because he too was clonked by the wrecking ball, still swinging wildly out of control. He went soaring like a discus across the pavilion. Finally, the wrecking ball smashed through the side wall of Petrified Pavilion and went rolling across the school yard, flattening the slide, the monkey bars, and the merry-go-round.

The kids' mouths hung open, and almost everyone was crying.

At that point, all the goblins rushed back onto the stage and started bowing and celebrating. They clearly thought they had put on a wonderful performance.

No one was clapping for them, but that didn't stop the goblins from cheering for themselves. It was very creepy.

Eventually the curtain fell so no one could see the goblins anymore, and *then* everyone finally started clapping.

Principal Headcrusher took the stage and said, "Okay . . . that was . . . interesting, right?"

All the kids booed.

"Fine, it was awful, so let's forget about it and get to the costume contest. The finalists for the two best costumes are . . . Fred Kroger and Charles Nukid!"

Everyone rolled their eyes because Fred and Charles were the only two kids wearing costumes.

Dr. Dragonbreath flew onto the stage and said, "Since the prize is a ride with me, I get to decide the winner. I say the winner is Fred."

All the kids cheered. Fred was back to being the school hero once again.

"What?" exclaimed Charles Nukid. "My outfit is much more scary and creative! Fred is just wearing a Viking helmet and holding a stick that's supposed to be some kind of spear. That's not even close to what dragon hunters wear. I'm Rule Number Five!"

"Listen," said Dr. Dragonbreath, "to be honest, your incessant rule following is very annoying. I'd rather not spend another second with you than I have to."

"But . . . but . . ."

Charles's words were too little too late. Now that he was no longer the school hero from his lunchtime success, everyone forgot Charles Nukid's name and he went back to being called "new kid," which was fine with him because he thought everyone was still calling him by his last name.

Principal Headcrusher raised her hands to her mouth and announced, "To conclude this very special Halloween, the Ghoul Games chairman, Franz Dietrich Wolfbark, would like to offer you a very special Halloween greeting."

A screen lowered from the ceiling, and the giant head of Mr. Wolfbark appeared on it. Makeup artists powdering his face quickly dashed out of the frame.

"Greetings, children of Scary School." Wolfbark spoke in a deep, ominous tone. "I have just been informed that your principal has allowed a gaggle of goblins to perform a Halloween play for you. Performing their awful shows is what makes goblins most happy. Unfortunately for you, goblins are considered the cockroaches of the monster world, and goblins being happy makes us monsters very *un*happy. I'm afraid I have no choice but to inform the monster community of this transgression, and now it is certain that none of you stand a chance of surviving the Ghoul Games."

There were some groans, but most of the kids had already given up hope, and they rolled their eyes at yet another reason why the Ghoul Games would be their untimely end.

Wolfbark concluded by proclaiming, "Have a happy Halloween, and I hope none of you eat any poison candy, because I wouldn't want to miss the opportunity of watching any of you being eaten alive at the Ghoul Games this spring. Turn off the camera!"

Principal Headcrusher loosened her collar and muttered, "Oh yeah, I forgot about that whole goblin thing. Sorry, kids."

About two hundred kids slapped their hands on their foreheads at the same time.

After the costume contest, the rest of Ms. Fang's class went back to the classroom to finish the hockey game. They even convinced Ms. Fang to join in, and she was having a wonderful time.

The only snag in the day came when Ms. Fang tripped over Penny Possum and her hockey stick plunged straight into the chest of Benny Porter, the kid vampire.

"Oopsy!" Ms. Fang said.

Benny Porter shriveled up and died right there on

the floor with a hockey stake through his heart.

"I'm so sorry, Benny."

He was the first kid Ms. Fang
had killed all year.
Ironically, it was on the
one day when everyone was
the safest and no kid was supposed to die, but
accidents do happen. Benny learned a very important
life lesson about not playing hockey indoors, unless, of
course, you happen to be playing indoor hockey.

Ms. Fang sounded an alarm, and once again Nurse
Hairymoles appeared in the room in a puff of smoke.

"Oh great," said Nurse Hairymoles. "Now
I'm going to have to spend my Halloween night turning this kid
into a zombie. And I had
so many poison apples
I planned on
handing out."

WOO
HOO!

After school, Fred rode on Dr. Dragonbreath's back as
he did his patrol over Goblin Hill. When they
got to the top, they saw the goblin actors
from the show attacking
Mr. Turtlesnaps.

They were hacking at his shell with tiny axes, yelling, "Turtle soup! Turtle soup! Turtle soup!"

Dr. Dragonbreath swooped down and blew a stream of fire that covered the whole hill. The goblins burst into flames and ran down the hill screaming, then jumped into Gremlin River to put themselves out.

Mr. Turtlesnaps poked his head out and waved "thanks" to them.

"Wow!" said Fred. "*This* is the best dream ever!"

13

Mrs. T Tricks a Dodo

Mrs. T is the Scary School detention monitor and also the school librarian.

She was born in a laboratory on a faraway island where scientists were growing dinosaurs for an insane billionaire who wanted them roaming around his backyard to impress his insane billionaire friends.

Mrs. T didn't have a brain the size of a peanut like most other T. rexes. Due to a DNA mix-up, she had an enormous brain that made her smarter than any human alive.

Because she was so smart, the last thing she wanted to be was some insane billionaire's pet, so she hatched a dastardly plan that ended in all the backyard dinosaurs rampaging the billionaire's mansion, eating the billionaire, and stealing his private jet. The billionaire learned a very important life lesson about not keeping man-eating dinosaurs as pets.

Mrs. T used the billionaire's jet to travel all over the world and learn new things everywhere she went. After twenty years of traveling, she could speak every language on Earth.

Mrs. T wore the same blue dress and blue hat every day because in all her travels around the world, it was the only outfit she had ever found that was her size.

Mrs. T loved to read and learn new things more than anything else. The problem was that her tiny arms were so short, she couldn't hold a book far enough away for her eyes to see it. So, she had to rely on others to read to her, which people usually did when she asked, because who's going to say no to a T. rex in a blue dress?

As she entered her twilight years, she decided to settle down and enjoy the quiet life working at Scary School. She took good care of the library. It was always nice and quiet, mainly because if anyone was loud, she just walked over and ate them, and that was the end of the disturbance.

While working at Scary School, she also met the love of her life, Mr. Spider-Eyes, and they got married. She liked him because his hundreds of eyes made it impossible for him to read a book, so he never tried to impress her with his intelligence, because he didn't have much of it.

They are a very good team. As the hall monitor, Mr. Spider-Eyes sends Mrs. T all the rule breakers he can find. When a rule breaker goes to detention, Mrs. T makes them read to her until lunchtime.

To give the kids a chance, detention never lasts past lunch, but if a kid accidentally stays too long, he is plain out of luck and Mrs. T has a very easy lunch for herself. Normally, at noon sharp, Mrs. T lets out a loud roar because she is so hungry, and then she stomps into Scary Forest to catch her lunch and also bring something back for Sue the Amazing Octo-Chef to prepare for the students.

One day, Sue asked Mrs. T to bring back a plump dodo bird from Scary Forest so she could add it to her special Thanksgiving-week menu. It made sense since dodoes are kind of like gigantic turkeys, only much more extinct.

"I want to give the kids an extra-special meal this Thanksgiving," gurgled Sue the Amazing Octo-Chef

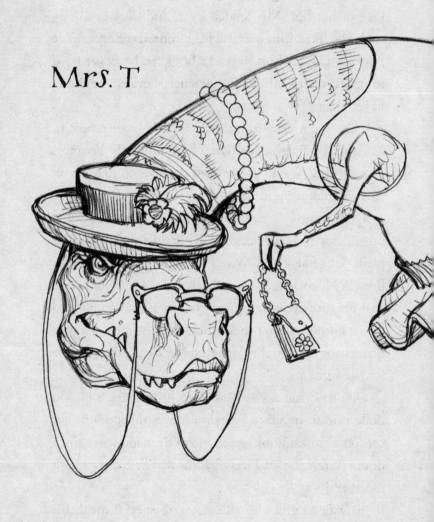

Mrs. T

from inside her tank. "After the Ghoul Games this spring, the students may not live to see another Thanksgiving, and I hear dodoes are the most delicious, must succulent birds there ever were."

"I hate to break this to you, Sue," said Mrs. T, "but dodoes went extinct over three hundred years ago."

"Well, I hate to break this to *you*," Sue replied, "but dinosaurs went extinct over sixty-five *million* years ago, and yet here you are standing in front of me."

"Good point," said Mrs. T. "I'll see what I can find."

And so at noon, Mrs. T let out her mighty roar and went galumphing into Scary Forest. Scary Forest has a way of helping visitors find what they need. The only problem is that once you find it, things can become very tricky. Scary Forest doesn't like to let go of its inhabitants.

As soon as Mrs. T entered Scary Forest, the trees lifted themselves from the ground and scampered in all directions as if their roots were tiny feet. The trees began whispering to one another in the Language of the Wind, which Mrs. T spoke very well.

Mrs. T whispered to the trees that she was looking for a dodo. The trees whispered to one another then lined up in two rows, forming a pathway for Mrs. T.

"Thank you," said Mrs. T, which sounded like a

whoosh and a rustle in the Language of the Wind.

Mrs. T followed the path until she came to a clearing. There was a big sign that said:

> *Welcome to Dodo Country—*
> *IQs under 200 need not enter.*

Mrs. T could hardly believe her eyes. There were hundreds of dodoes walking around. Each of them was between three and four feet tall and wearing professors' gowns and glasses. They held books between the feathers of their wings. Some of them were in groups discussing and debating the books they were holding.

Wow, thought Mrs. T. These are some smart dodoes.

Mrs. T walked out of the shadows into the clearing, looking for the plumpest dodo she could find.

The dodoes gasped when they saw the giant T. rex wearing a blue dress, but they didn't run. Instead they shouted, "It's her! It's her!" And they all ran up to her and knelt at her feet.

A dodo wearing thick glasses proclaimed, "We are very excited to see you. My name is Plato. Just as the prophecy foretold, the Great Ancestor has returned!"

"Great Ancestor? What are you talking about?" Mrs. T asked.

"Follow us!" said Plato the dodo.

Mrs. T followed the dodoes into a big building with a sign that said DODO HISTORY MUSEUM.

Painted on the inside wall was a gigantic diagram of the dodo family tree. It traced dodo lineage all the way back to the beginning, and at the very top was a picture of . . . Mrs. T?

"Hey, what's that picture of *me* doing on the wall?" Mrs. T inquired.

"You see," said Plato, "over sixty-five million years ago, you were the first dinosaur born with a giant brain. You invented writing and reading! All of your offspring were born with giant brains as well, and then over millions of years, your dinosaur descendants evolved into us dodoes, the smartest creatures on Earth. We lived happily on the paradise island of Mauritius just east of Madagascar for thousands of years, until humans discovered us. The humans realized that aside from being smart, we were even more delicious. It's not our fault we're so succulent! The humans hunted us to near extinction, so we left Mauritius and settled in Scary Forest, where no one could ever find us again. Here, we are free to read and write and philosophize to our heart's content."

"Wow, this place sounds like heaven," said Mrs. T. "But I thought the scientists who found my DNA and brought me back to life gave me my big brain."

"That's just what they thought happened because they couldn't explain it. The truth is, you were already smart and lived an incredible life. It's too bad you don't keep any of your memories when they regrow you from your DNA, or you'd remember all the amazing things you did. Luckily, you wrote it all down in your autobiography and even foretold that you would return to teach us all a very important lesson. We've been waiting millions of years for your return and are very eager to learn our lesson."

"Hmm. I have no clue what that lesson could possibly be," said Mrs. T. "You seem to know even more than I do about the world."

"That's what I've been saying all my life!" said Plato. "We don't need any lesson from some ancient dinosaur. We already know everything!"

"That settles that then," said Mrs. T, "but I still need to take one of you back with me for the school's lunch."

"No! You can't!" exclaimed Plato. "If humans find out we still exist, they'll start hunting us again and we really will go extinct!"

"Not if scientists find your DNA and bring you back, like they did with me."

"But . . . but . . . we're family! You wouldn't eat your own family, would you?"

"It's not me who would eat you; the kids would eat you. And *family* is a very loose term. If you go back far enough, *everyone* is family."

"I can't argue with that logic," said Plato. "If you have to take one of us, take Elbert—he's only written three literary masterpieces and solved two dilemmas of particle physics. He's a real slacker."

"Hey!" clucked Elbert.

Mrs. T didn't like Plato's attitude so she took him in her jaws, galumphed out of the forest, and brought him to Sue the Amazing Octo-Chef to cook for lunch.

As it turned out, Plato did learn his lesson, only it was too late.

Sue brought Plato out on a big plate, and when the students tasted the roast dodo, they immediately spat it out in disgust.

"Blech! That's the worst thing I've ever tasted!" said Ramon. "It tastes like a sweaty sock wrapped in snail goo." His opinion was seconded, thirded, and fourthed by each student who tried it.

"How strange," said Sue. "Legend says they went extinct because they were so delicious."

"I have a new theory on that," said Mrs. T. "I'm fairly certain they were hunted to extinction because they were such insufferable know-it-alls."

14
The Three Rs

At your school, "the three *R*s" probably stands for Reading, wRiting, and aRithmetic, but at Scary School, "the three *R*s" stands for Rachael, Raychel, and FRank (which is pronounced "Rachel").

While we're on the subject, why in the world do they call reading, writing, and arithmetic "the three *R*s?" I would understand if each word actually started with the letter *R*, but each word just happens to have an *R* in it. Isn't that ridiculous? You might as well just call it "the three *I*s" for readIng, wrIting, and arIthmetic, right?

Stickers!

Rachael

Also, why isn't it *reading, writing, and arithmeticking* . . . or *mathing*? Why can you read, but you can't math? When you think about it, this is a very bizarre language we speak, and the stupid people who speak it make it even worse by coming up with things like "the three *R*s" that confuse things even further. When you're a ghost, you have a lot of time to think about this stuff, and it drives you crazy.

Rachael is the tallest girl in Ms. Fang's class. She has long black hair and loves stickers. All her folders and textbooks are covered in stickers, her clothes are

Raychel

covered in stickers, and most of her stickers are covered in stickers.

Raychel is Rachael's best friend. She's the shortest girl in Ms. Fang's class. She has short blond hair and hates stickers. In fact, she hates anything that's sticky—glue, gum, honey, you name it. Three years ago she got gum caught in her hair and hasn't been able to get it out yet.

Rachael and Raychel don't have anything in common except for the pronunciation of their names, but that's enough for them to be best friends.

Frank, which is pronounced "Rachel," is the exact middle in height in Ms. Fang's class. Since Benny died, she is the fifteenth tallest one, or the fifteenth shortest one depending on your perspective. There are fourteen kids shorter than her and fourteen kids taller than her in the class. She has frizzy brown hair and loves jumping rope. She used to jump rope all day every day. She would jump rope on her way to class, jump rope eating lunch, and would even fall asleep jumping rope at night. One morning she woke up and the automatic counter on her jump rope was at two million jumps!

At the end of last year, Frank lost control of her jump rope and it flew through the air and poked Mr. Spider-Eyes in twenty of his eyes. Using Monster Math, that's almost eighteen thousand eyes. He got angry and took Frank's jump rope away. Now Frank hops down the halls jumping an imaginary rope.

Frank's only friend is Petunia, but everyone thinks that her friends are Rachael and Raychel since she's one of the three Rachels. The truth is, Rachael and Raychel won't let Frank be their friend because they don't like the way Frank spells her name. People

Imaginary Jump rope!

FIP FIP
FIP FIP

HOP TO IT!

FIP

FIP

FIP

FIP
FIP
FIP

FIP

FIP

Frank

thought Frank's parents must not have been able to read, but that isn't true, either.

Frank's parents come from Gnomania. In Gnomania, *F*s are pronounced like *R*s, *R*s are silent, *A*s are the same, and *NK* is pronounced "chel." Thus, "Frank" is how they spell "Rachel."

I sure used a lot of quotation marks in that last paragraph. I wonder what a paragraph would look like if it were nothing but quotation marks. Let's try it.

"""""" """""""""" """"""""""""""" """""""""""""""""""""""""""""".
"""""""""""""""""""""""""""" """"" """"""""""""""""""""""""
"""""""" """"""""""""""""""""""""""""""""""""""" """"""""""""""""""""""
"""""""""""""""""""""""""""""""? """"""""""""""""""""""""""""
"" """"""""""""""""""""! """""" """""
"""""""""""""""""""""""""""" """"""""""""""""".

Okay, that was stupid. But hey, I'm a ghost. I get bored very easily.

It was getting close to winter vacation, and Rachael and Raychel were practicing extra hard for the Ghoul Games. They decided to join together as a team for their chosen game.

They saw Frank at the end of the yard skipping imaginary rope all by herself. They called out to her, "Hey, Frank, come over and play with us!"

"Okay!" said Frank, very excited someone wanted to play with her. She dropped her imaginary rope and

151

ran over to Rachael and Raychel. "What game are we playing?"

"What are you doing here, Frank?" said Rachael with a sneer.

"Yeah, we don't want to play with *you*," said Raychel, even sneerier.

"Oh . . . I thought you . . . never mind," said Frank, and she hung her head and walked back to her imaginary jump rope.

The two Rachels called out to her again. "Hey, Frank, we were just kidding! Come over here and play with us!"

Frank dropped her rope again and ran over to the Rachels.

"I totally knew you were kidding," said Frank. "What are we playing?"

"Eww! As if we'd ever play a game with someone who spells their name like *you* do," said Rachael.

"Yeah, why don't you go play with Petunia or one of the other freaks and leave us alone?" said Raychel.

"Are you kidding again?" asked Frank.

"No," said Rachael.

"Yes," said Raychel.

"Yes," said Rachael.

"No," said Raychel.

Frank just stared at them for a few moments while

they sneered at her, then smiled, then sneered, then smiled, then sneered. Eventually she just ran off crying.

"Wow," said Rachael, "we are getting really good at these mind games."

"Yeah, I'm really glad we chose mind games for our Ghoul Games event."

"I'm not. Yes I am. No I'm not. . . ."

Recess ended, and the two Rachels started walking back to class, but they tripped and fell to the ground, and everyone laughed at them.

"Why do our legs feel tied together?" the two Rachels asked each other.

From across the yard, Frank thought to herself, wow, I'm getting really good at tying these imaginary ropes.

15

Mr. Snakeskin

The last day of school before winter break is a very special day.

All the hard tests are over, and the whole day is more like a big party than a day at school. Ms. Fang's class was especially excited and had been waiting all year for this day. Today was the day that Mr. Snakeskin would be visiting their class to give them a lesson in human biology.

How could a class be excited about a biology lesson? I'll tell you. Mr. Snakeskin was a sixth-grade teacher; however, the sixth graders were old enough to have a holiday party all by themselves, so Mr. Snakeskin left them with their party and walked into Ms. Fang's fifth-grade classroom, where the kids were anxiously waiting for him.

He was a tall man with short brown hair. He coached all the sports teams and looked pretty much like you would expect a guy who coached all the sports teams to look.

The thing with Mr. Snakeskin is that he's half human, half zombie, so that means he's half alive, half dead. When you're half dead, you can do all sorts of things you *can't* do when you're fully alive. One of those things is to give biology lessons in his unique way.

When he walked in, Mr. Snakeskin was wearing his Scary School Basketball sweatshirt.

"Good afternoon," said Mr. Snakeskin in his strong, authoritative voice. "I'm here to give you all a lesson in biology that you will never forget. Indeed, I can promise that after this lesson, you will all be experts in the subject of human anatomy."

At that, Mr. Snakeskin reached down and pulled his sweatshirt over his head. When he did that, he not only pulled off his sweatshirt, but all of his skin, too!

The class yelled, "Whooooa!" as they saw what the inside of a body looks like for the first time. It was a

Mr. Snakeskin

mass of muscles and organs that looked totally gross and weird.

"I can tell you think I look totally gross and weird," said Mr. Snakeskin, "but you would do well to remember that each of you looks exactly the same under your skin, too!"

"How can you do that?" asked Ramon. "I'm a zombie and I can't do that."

"Because I'm only half zombie. To put it simply, I'm still human on the inside, but zombie on the outside. If I were one hundred percent alive, I would be shrieking in pain. If I were one hundred percent dead, all my insides would rot away and disintegrate in an instant."

"That would be cool," said Johnny.

"Let's begin our lesson then," Mr. Snakeskin continued. "There are many hundreds of muscles that make movement possible. Starting at the arms, there are the biceps, triceps, deltoids, and your finger flexors. Moving across, we have the pectoral muscles, the latissimus dorsi muscles, the obliques, and the abdominal muscles. Playing sports and exercising keeps all of these muscles strong and healthy, but sitting in front of the TV and playing video games makes them wither away and shrink, so get out there and exercise as much as you can!"

"Does sitting down and doing homework make your muscles shrink, too?" asked Fritz, a skinny boy who always wore swimming goggles. More about him in the next book.

"Yes," replied Mr. Snakeskin. "That's why you should always do fifty jumping jacks after every math problem you finish."

Ms. Fang interjected, "He's just kidding, class. That would be silly."

"Of course I was just kidding," said Mr. Snakeskin. "Doing fifty jumping jacks would be very silly. Hardly a workout. You should do fifty push-ups. Moving right along to the organs . . ."

Mr. Snakeskin proceeded to pull off all of his muscles, so now the class could see his inner organs and guts. Some kids retched, some kids fainted, some kids barfed, but most of them cheered.

Mr. Snakeskin continued, "First will be a demonstration of the digestive system."

Ms. Fang tossed Mr. Snakeskin a small holiday cupcake, and he caught it in his mouth.

As he chewed the cupcake, Mr. Snakeskin explained, "This cupcake is already being predigested by the saliva in my mouth. As I swallow, it passes down this tube called the esophagus and makes its way into my stomach, where the digestion continues. After the stomach is done breaking the cupcake down, it goes into this series of tubes called the small intestine, where it will be broken down into nutrients for my body to use. After that, only the unusable stuff is left, and it travels into this long tube called the large intestine, where it waits patiently until you ask Ms. Fang for a restroom pass."

The class cheered again.

"There are many more systems of the body that do some amazing things. These two large pink sacs are my lungs, which are controlling my respiratory system. When we breathe in the air around us, our bodies extract the oxygen we need, and then we exhale the carbon dioxide we don't need. This big slab is my liver, which is filtering out all the bad stuff that my body doesn't want. These bones in my chest make up my rib cage, which protects my heart and lungs."

Then Mr. Snakeskin pulled apart his ribs so that the class could see his heart!

"Who wants to come up and feel my heart beating?"

The class jumped out of their seats and lined up. Each student reached out tentatively and felt Mr. Snakeskin's heart as it pumped in and out at a constant rate.

"The heart is controlling my circulatory system,

pumping blood all over the body, delivering nutrients where they need to go, fighting diseases, and maintaining a steady body temperature. Remember, don't any of you try anything close to this, or you would die instantly."

"Well, duh," said Rachael and Raychel.

When everyone had felt his heart, he closed his ribs back up, reattached all his muscles like putting on a suit, then put on his sweatshirt and was back to normal.

The class clapped for him. As he bowed, he took off the top of his head and exposed his brains to everyone.

"Oops!" he said. "That's for your next lesson."

"Class," said Ms. Fang, "before you all leave, I want to wish you a wonderful and fun winter vacation, but I would advise you to think about what you've learned so far at Scary School and what it means to you. Also, I encourage all of you to spend your free time practicing for your Ghoul Games event if you want to have the least hope of survival. Class dismissed. Have a very happy holiday break!"

The kids cheered with the sheer exhilaration and freedom of the moment and rushed out to the parking lot, where their parents were waiting for them.

"You know what I learned?" Petunia said to Frank as they ran down the hall.

"What?"

"People are a lot like presents. It's what's on the inside that counts."

16

Johnny, Ramon, and Peter's Disgusting Idea

For the Ghoul Games, Johnny, Ramon, and Peter decided to play together as a three-man basketball team. Johnny, Ramon, and Peter are best friends and each one of them also happens to be a Scary kid.

Johnny is a Sasquatch, but when his feet grow enough, he'll be a Bigfoot. You may remember from before that Johnny has messy brown hair. That is true, except the messy brown hair is *everywhere*. The only part of him that doesn't have hair on it is his nose, which is big and round like a clown's nose, and has a small red freckle on the end of it. Johnny is very protective of his one freckle, but the truth is that his face is covered in freckles. He just can't see them because of all the hair.

Ramon is a kid zombie. That means he is a living mind inside of a dead, decaying body. Parts of his body are always falling off, usually his fingers, toes, and ears. Whenever a kid sees a random body part lying in the hallway or on the playground, they always bring it back to Ramon, and he puts it back on with glue. In order to keep his zombie brain alive, he needs to eat brains. Any kind of brains will do; even a whole handful of bug brains or fish brains will get the job done. People brains are a very special treat.

Peter, as you may remember, is a werewolf. When Peter is a regular kid, he is called Peter and is the nicest kid in school. When Peter is a wolf, he is called

Ramon

Johnny

Peter

Peter the Wolf and turns into the meanest kid in school. At the age of ten, he has no control yet over when he turns into a wolf. Kids try to be extra nice to him, but if the slightest thing doesn't go his way, he becomes Peter the Wolf and everyone better watch out.

Johnny, Ramon, and Peter are a very good basket-ball team because each has a different skill. Johnny the Sasquatch is the tallest kid in class, so he gets all the rebounds and makes good passes. Ramon the zombie is a "dead-on" shot, so he drains three-pointers like they're layups. When Peter is just Peter, he's awful. When Peter is Peter the Wolf, he can jump ten feet in the air, so he likes to jump over people and dunk.

The only problem is Peter's claws sometimes pop the ball, so he has to keep them filed or else the game is over as soon as he touches the ball.

After winter break, the three of them practiced basketball every day during recess and even after school. Since there were three of them, they always had to play two against one. Whoever was the "one" would always get creamed. The first week of practice, Johnny and Ramon beat Peter 98 to 4. Peter and Ramon beat Johnny 77 to 12. Johnny and Peter beat Ramon 145 to 3.

Using Monster Math, Ramon lost 243 billion to negative 6 trillion.

They kept practicing, playing two against one every day, and then an amazing thing started to happen. The "one" player had to work so hard just to stay in the game that all three improved much faster than normal. After just three weeks, the two-on-ones became almost dead-even matches. Johnny and Ramon beat

Peter 56 to 53. Peter and Ramon beat Johnny 65 to 64 (Ramon hit a lucky three-pointer at the buzzer to pull it out). Ramon actually beat Johnny and Peter 82 to 74. That game Ramon got a very hot hand, which was technically always cold.

All three were at the top of their games and felt unstoppable. They couldn't wait for the Ghoul Games to start. Until, that is, they got a greeting card from their opponents.

Scream Academy was sending their star basketball players to play against them. The greeting card showed each player standing next to a basketball hoop.

"Oh nuts," said Johnny, Ramon, and Peter as they looked at the card.

Their opponents were *giants*. Literally.

Each one was in fifth grade like they were, but they were at least eight feet tall. They looked like they could dunk without even jumping. Johnny was the tallest kid in Ms. Fang's class, but he was only five feet tall.

"What are we going to do, guys?" asked Johnny, quivering.

"I don't know," said Ramon. "If I eat some big brains, maybe I can figure something out."

"I could stop filing my claws down," said Peter. "If I get the ball early, I can pop the ball and then maybe we'll have a zero-zero tie."

"Come on, there has to be a way," said Johnny. "It's just like math . . . there's always a right answer."

"We could play on sti—," Ramon tried to say, but his tongue fell out of his mouth and landed on the ground. He brushed it off and put it back in his mouth. "Sorry. We could play on stilts."

"I have a feeling that's a bad idea," said Peter.

"Yeah, I'm pretty sure that would be cheating," said Johnny.

"Wait, I got it," said Johnny. "Let's eat really gross, disgusting bugs every day until the Ghoul Games. That way, when the giants eat us, we'll taste as gross as the bugs, and maybe they'll spit us out."

"I think that's the best plan we're gonna get," said Johnny.

"I agree," said Peter.

So they started running around the school yard looking for insects to eat.

"There's one!" said Johnny, pointing to a flying beetle.

Ramon saw it flying in the air, and he heaved the basketball at it from twenty feet away. Of course it was a perfect shot. The ball hit the beetle in the air and knocked it out. The beetle fell toward the ground, and

Johnny ran underneath it and caught it on the rebound. Johnny passed the beetle to Peter, who dunked it in some ketchup, and together they enjoyed a disgusting beetle snack.

"This tastes terrible!" said Ramon.

"I know, it's perfect," said Johnny. "If we taste half this bad, we're home free."

"I think it's pretty good," said Peter the Wolf. "If you guys taste half this good, I might eat you before the giants do."

17

Jason's Mask

Jason loves two things in life. One is hockey. The second we'll get to in a moment.

Jason is the goalie for the Scary School hockey team. He is very good at it and almost never allows a goal. Last year, Scary School won the league hockey championship, barely defeating Adventure School, 2–1. Jason was the MVP of the team and got a huge trophy. He was sure Scary School would win the hockey tournament during the Ghoul Games in the spring and he practiced every day for it.

I don't care how big those monsters are, he thought

to himself. They're not getting the puck past me.

As Jason was daydreaming, Peter hit a puck right past him for an easy goal.

The second thing Jason loves is his teacher, Ms. Fang. He thinks she is the most beautiful woman, human or vampire, ever to walk this Earth. Jason is one of the smartest kids in class, but sometimes he does poorly on his homework so that Ms. Fang will ask him to stay after class and give him an extra lesson. When he aces it on the second try, it makes Ms. Fang happy that she did such a good job teaching him, even though he secretly knew the answers already.

There was a precise moment when Jason fell for Ms. Fang. He had just finished playing hockey during lunch and rushed to class. If he walked in late, he knew Ms. Fang would bite his neck, and that would be the end of him. He made it to class just in time, but he was in such a hurry that he had forgotten to take off his goalie mask.

Ms. Fang pulled down an unmarked map.

"Okay, class," she said, "who wants to come up to the map and name every country in Eastern Europe?"

Jason knew those countries by heart because he had traveled through Eastern Europe on vacation that summer. Jason's hand flew up along with several other kids'—Wendy's, Lefty's, and Maria's. This bothered

Jason, and he tried to raise
his hand extra high.

Ms. Fang scanned
the room and was
about to call on Jason.
However, her brain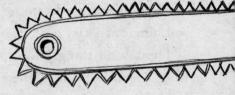
had already reached the maximum number of names
it could hold, and she couldn't remember Jason's name.
So what she said instead was, "You. The handsome
kid."

Jason lowered his hand and was extremely disappointed. Then Fred poked him. "Jason, she means
you."

"Huh?" Jason had never been called handsome
before and was not used to it. The years of hockey
pucks flying at his face had disfigured him pretty
badly. His nose looked like a walnut, and he had very
few teeth to speak of.

Ms. Fang got frustrated and pointed her pointer
at Jason. "I don't have all day," she bellowed. "Just
because you're the handsomest boy in class, don't
think you can waste everyone's time."

That was the moment.

Jason leaped out of his chair like a kangaroo, but his
heart leaped even higher. She thinks I'm handsome!
he thought to himself. Then, he put his hands to his

Jason

face and felt the
white goalie mask.

Oh no, he
realized. I'm still
wearing the goalie
mask. He was about
to pull it off, but then
noticed Ms. Fang smile at
him. His train of thought continued:
She thinks the hockey mask is
my face. That's why she
thinks I'm handsome.

Rather than being
bothered by that, that
made Jason feel happy.
He thought, if it's so easy

to make myself handsome, I should have done this years ago!

Unfortunately, all this thinking to himself was being done while he was supposed to be naming all the countries in Eastern Europe, and he got completely flustered and mixed them all up. He didn't get one of them right.

"Well, you have guts," said Ms. Fang, "but stay after class so we can review this."

Jason smiled, but of course nobody saw it.

Jason sat down with Ms. Fang after class and he still hadn't stopped smiling.

"Now, pay attention," Ms. Fang said. She named all the countries in Eastern Europe. As soon as she finished, Jason stepped forward and named them back just as perfectly.

"Wow! I really am a great teacher!" Ms. Fang proclaimed with a big smile. "And you get a gold star for the day."

Jason was feeling fantastic. Maybe a little too fantastic, or he would never have had the confidence to say what he said next.

"Ms. Fang, can I ask you question?"

"Sure."

"Will you marry me?"

Ms. Fang burst into laughter, which Jason found rather insulting.

"Don't be silly. There's no way I could marry you."

"Why not?" Jason asked.

"For one thing, you're human and I'm a vampire, and second, I'm eight hundred and fifty years old and you're ten."

"I'm almost eleven," Jason said hopefully.

"Forget about it. You're not at all the type of man I would marry."

"What type of man is that?"

"Not a kid like you, that's for sure. Is it too much to ask for a gentleman vampire who's at least nine hundred years old and could afford to buy me a brand-new cherrywood coffin to sleep in? I sure hope someone like that comes soon, 'cause my old coffin has dry rot you wouldn't believe. Now you get on home . . . um . . ."

"Jason. My name is Jason."

Jason walked home and still kept his mask on. No one could see him crying.

Two weeks later was Jason's eleventh birthday. He opened his present from his dad, and inside was a brand-new chainsaw.

Jason's dad was a lumberjack and cut down the trees around their house and sold the wood to support the family. He was hoping Jason would take to it and join the family business.

Father and son went out together, and sure enough, Jason took to it. It took some practice, but in no time he was sawing down trees just as fast as his dad. Soon, he became the best chainsaw wielder anyone had ever seen. He even took it a step further and taught himself to carve wood as well as anyone ever has.

That winter, Jason skipped hockey practice on weekends so he could spend all his spare time working on a special tree he'd found. He still kept the goalie mask on and would for the rest of his life.

On February 14, Valentine's Day morning, Ms. Fang woke up to find a brand-new, beautifully carved cherrywood coffin sitting on her doorstep.

There was no note.

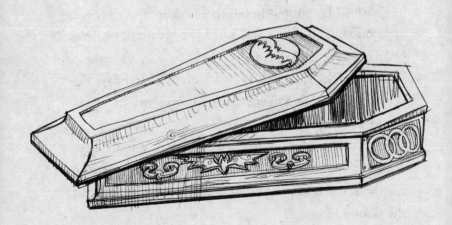

18
Scary Garden

Following Valentine's Day, Ms. Fang seemed to be getting much better sleep and thus was always in a much better mood. The class drew pictures of sunshine all over the boarded-up windows, which made the classroom feel bright and cheery.

When the first day of spring came on March 21, Ms. Fang asked for a volunteer to walk across the school yard to Scary Garden to pick a batch of spring flowers for the classroom.

Jason raised his hand immediately.

Ms. Fang said, "Thank you, Jason. Your chainsaw

should be very useful in case something goes wrong there, but I would also like a girl with good taste in flowers to go. How about you, Lindsey?"

"Um, can't you tell I just got a new haircut?" said Lindsey, rolling her eyes. "I'm not going outside where the wind will mess it up."

"Sorry I asked. Petunia, how about you?"

"As long as I don't have to pick any petunias," said Petunia. "I hate petunias."

"Yes, that fine. Now we have two. Anyone else?"

As soon as they saw Petunia was going, Johnny, Ramon, and Peter raised their hands.

"Okay, Johnny, why don't you go? Since you're the tallest, you can reach higher for flowers hanging off of trees."

Peter quickly turned into Peter the Wolf and barked, "But I can jump ten feet in the air when I'm a wolf!"

"But if I choose you to go, Peter, you will have gotten your way and will turn back into regular Peter, and then you won't be much use at all."

Peter growled to himself and crossed his arms.

Ms. Fang continued, "I need one more girl to go in case something happens to Petunia."

Frank (which is pronounced "Rachel"), Petunia's only friend, raised her hand.

"Thank you, Frank," said Ms. Fang. "That should be enough. To make it fun, whoever can make it back alive in under an hour gets a homework pass."

The class groaned. If they had known they would get a homework pass, everyone would have volunteered, even if it meant risking their lives.

Jason, Petunia, Johnny, and Frank walked down the hallway toward the school yard. Scary Garden was at the end of the school yard behind a tall white fence that prevented the dangerous plants from attacking the students. There were holes in the fence that kids had to watch out for, because sometimes a hungry plant would reach through the hole to snatch a good meal. But that didn't happen *too* often.

As they walked down the hallway, Frank was skipping her invisible jump rope and counting out loud. "One thousand five hundred sixty-six, one thousand five hundred sixty-seven, one thousand five hundred sixty-eight . . ."

Johnny was walking next to Petunia.

"Don't walk so close," said Petunia to Johnny. "I don't want to catch your fleas."

"But I just had a flea bath last night," said Johnny.

Jason groaned, "Frank! Will you please stop jumping rope? You're going to distract us."

"Whatever," said Frank. "Unlike some, I'm actually

practicing for the Ghoul Games. I don't plan on being eaten."

"Well, if you're not careful, you're going to get eaten right now," said Jason. "Making it across the school yard at this hour is no guarantee."

They stood at the back door together, looking out into the school yard. They all became nervous, like the moment before jumping out of a plane when sky-diving.

"Well, let's do this," said Jason.

The four began walking across the school yard, which was eerily quiet without any kids running around. To their left was the playground equipment, which the goblins had spent the last three months rebuilding after their wrecking ball smashed everything on Halloween. To their right, they saw what looked like a house under construction. A third-grade girl named Jacqueline was on the roof hammering nails.

"What are you doing?" shouted Petunia.

"I'm building a haunted house for my brother, Derek the Ghost," Jacqueline yelled back. "Right now he's a homeless ghost with no place to haunt."

"You're lucky. I wish *my* brother were a ghost," Jason replied.

The four students continued walking by the play-ground—one of the most fun areas of Scary School, but also one of the most deadly. There is going to be a *lot* more about it in the next book. Since the goblins had rebuilt the playground, the students of Scary School had the distinct feeling that the goblins were trying to get rid of them so they could expand their territory beyond Goblin Hill.

The foursome marched past the Monkey Bars of Doom, at least thirty feet high and suspended over a pool of bubbling hot lava. You do *not* want to lose your grip on those monkey bars. Next, they strolled past the possessed merry-go-round. If you're brave enough to get on that thing, you better hold on tight, because the evil spirit that possesses it doesn't like to be ridden. It will spin you so fast, you could go flying off it and land hundreds of feet away. And if that happens, you better pray you don't land in the quicksand box or the snake pit or the crocodile farm or the well of a thousand screams or the . . . okay, you get the point.

Jason, Petunia, Frank, and Johnny deftly avoided all of the horrible traps of the school yard, but as they rounded past the sinister swing set, a chill ran up each of their spines. They were standing in front of Petrified Pavilion and had been spotted by the gargoyles perched atop the highest branches.

"Look at 'em!" said Gary the gargoyle. "They're

not supposed to be out of class. Let's get 'em!"

"Argh, it doesn't look like they're coming into the pavilion, Gary," said Larry the gargoyle.

"Who cares? They're rule breakers anyway. I'm starving!" said Gary.

"I'm convinced," said Larry. "Let's go."

Larry and Gary the gargoyles banked off the pavilion and swooped down toward the children. As soon as they jumped, their brothers, Harry and Barry, also jumped off the roof and followed behind them.

"Heads up!" yelled Johnny, pointing at the four gargoyles flying swiftly toward them.

Gary the gargoyle zoomed

toward Jason. Jason turned on his chainsaw, and as Gary dove down to snatch him, Jason jumped up, and sliced the monstrous gargoyle in half with the chainsaw.

Larry zoomed toward Petunia, aiming to chomp off her head, but Petunia took her hat off, and a swarm of bees immediately flew in front of her and attacked Larry the gargoyle. Gargoyles are very allergic to bee stings, and Larry dropped dead on the spot.

Harry zoomed toward Frank, which is pronounced "Rachel." Frank took her imaginary jump rope and swung it at Harry. The imaginary rope wrapped around Harry's neck, and the gargoyle was strangled in midair and fell to the ground, dead.

Barry zoomed toward Johnny. Being a Sasquatch, Johnny was as strong as ten men and fierce as a lion. Barry was doomed from the start. Johnny grabbed the gargoyle by its scaly feet, spun around in circles, then hurled Barry up into the air like a Frisbee. He threw Barry so high, the poor gargoyle shot all the way into Earth's upper atmosphere, where he immediately froze into ice. Then he plummeted back down and landed with a thunk on top of Petrified Pavilion. Since Barry was frozen stiff as stone, he had actually turned into a regular gargoyle statue. The four gargoyles learned the very important life lesson that when something seems too good to be true, it usually is.

When the rest of the gargoyles saw what had happened to Gary, Larry, Harry, and Barry, they did not attack the students because they didn't want to suffer a similar fate. Instead, they dug graves with their claws, buried their brethren, then flew over the white fence into Scary Garden to gather flowers.

The gargoyles placed beautiful flowers on Gary's, Larry's, and Harry's graves before flying back to the pavilion.

"Hey," said Jason, looking at the graves, "check out these great flowers. If we take these back to Ms. Fang, we won't have to go into Scary Garden after all."

"Are you sure?" Petunia asked. "I really, really thought we were going to have a crazy adventure in Scary Garden."

"Yeah, me, too," said Johnny.

"I was sure of it," said Frank.

"Listen," said Jason, "we all thought we were going to go to Scary Garden, but why even bother? The gargoyles did the work for us."

"I guess things don't always go as planned," said Petunia.

"Will we go there later?" asked Johnny.

"How should I know? Who am I, Derek the Ghost?" Jason answered sarcastically.

Jason, Petunia, Frank, and Johnny took the flowers and brought them back to Ms. Fang's classroom. Ms. Fang was shocked that they had all made it back alive in less than ten minutes, and they all got homework passes. They were heroes for surviving Scary Garden.

None of them dared say what really happened.

19

Penny Possum

Penny Possum was the quietest girl in Ms. Fang's class. She hadn't said a word to anyone in over two years, and that was fine with her. She has short black hair and very large round eyes that give her extraordinary night vision.

Penny Possum has a unique way of surviving Scary School.

Whenever she's in trouble, she drops to the floor and plays dead. That way, the angry teacher or monster just ignores her, and she lives to see another day.

She was so good at it, she decided that playing

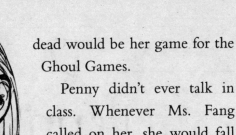

dead would be her game for the Ghoul Games.

Penny didn't ever talk in class. Whenever Ms. Fang called on her, she would fall over and pretend to die so that she wouldn't have to answer the question. The first few times, her parents had to come pick up her body, and then, to no one's surprise, she'd be back in school the next day. After the first week, Ms. Fang stopped calling on her.

One day, Ms. Fang asked Penny to deliver a note to Dr. Dragonbreath.

Penny walked into the room and interrupted Dr. Dragonbreath's lecture on the Dragon-Caveman Treaty of 30,000 BCE. Penny tried to hand him the note, but before she could, Dr. Dragonbreath said, "Before you speak, my dear, I would advise you to read the five rules on the board so that you don't say the

Penny

wrong thing, which might get you eaten."

Penny didn't plan on speaking, but she began reading the five rules anyway. Charles Nukid was waving at her, trying to warn her, but she didn't heed his warning and read Rule Number Five. She realized right away that she was in big trouble.

"I'm sorry, young girl. When you're in my classroom, you have to follow *all* my rules," said Dr. Dragonbreath, removing his glasses.

Dr. Dragonbreath's wings burst out of his shirt and he flew toward her, but when he reached her, he saw that she was already dead on the floor. He couldn't tell she was just pretending to be dead. Penny was even able to stop her heart from beating and make her body completely rigid so that it really appeared utterly lifeless.

"Oh my, the poor girl must have had a heart attack—I can't eat her now because she's not totally fresh. Dead humans are so chewy. Charles, will you please drag her out into the hall so she doesn't smell up the room?"

"Yes, sir," said Charles Nukid, and he dragged Penny out into the hallway. As soon as she was out the door, she took a deep breath and sprang up. Charles nearly passed out, he was so frightened, and he very quickly had to fix three hairs that sprang out of place.

Penny put her finger to her lips, telling Charles to keep quiet.

"Okay," said Charles, "I won't tell."

Penny handed Ms. Fang's note to Charles, then ran off.

The next day, Penny gave Charles a piece of hard candy to thank him for trying to warn her about Rule Number Five. Since she didn't speak when she gave it to him, Charles didn't know what the candy was for, so he brought her a piece of candy the next day as a thank-you. Penny didn't understand why he gave her the candy: she thought they were already even, so she brought him another candy the next day. Every day they gave each other a piece of candy, not sure exactly why they were doing it.

It was April Fool's Day at Scary School. The Ghoul Games were a little over a month away.

Penny Possum overheard some of her classmates saying they were going to play an April Fool's Day prank on "the new kid." She knew they meant Charles Nukid. They were going to convince him to go into Mr. Spider-Eyes's office, a place not many kids came out of alive if they were bad enough to get sent there.

As you may remember, Mr. Spider-Eyes is the strict hall monitor who has one hundred tiny eyes on each side of his head. His wife is Mrs. T. Because he has so many eyes, being in bright places for too long gives him a bad headache. He therefore keeps his office pitch dark, which is the perfect amount of light for him. Nobody is sure what his office looks like since he keeps it so dark.

During lunch, Stephanie, one of Lindsey's friends, handed Charles Nukid a note that said to report to Mr. Spider-Eyes's office immediately.

Great, thought Charles to himself. What did I do this time? Wear the wrong color socks?

Charles got up from the table and left the lunch hall for Mr. Spider-Eyes's office. All of Lindsey's friends started giggling to themselves. Penny Possum left her lunch and followed him out.

She considered Charles to be her only friend and didn't want anything bad to happen to him. Charles didn't consider Penny to be a friend. He thought she wouldn't talk to him because she didn't think he was cool enough. Since he wasn't in Ms. Fang's class, he had no idea she never spoke to *anybody*.

As Charles walked down the hallway, Penny ran in front of him and started jumping, waving her arms, and doing a dance to try to stop him, but he thought she was making fun of his skinny arms and kept walking.

When he got to Mr. Spider-Eyes's door, Penny

tried to pull him back, but Charles squirmed away and opened the door.

A rush of light poured in, Mr. Spider-Eyes hissed, and for a moment, Charles and Penny saw the figures of Mr. Spider-Eyes and another man, who was thin with gray hair and wore glasses and a drab gray suit. Charles and Penny did not recognize him in the dark, but you, my sharp readers, know him as Franz Dietrich Wolfbark, the chairman of the Ghoul Games.

"Close the door! Close the door!" shouted Mr. Spider-Eyes.

Charles went inside and closed the door behind him as Penny sneaked in with him at the last second.

It was pitch black inside and Charles couldn't see a thing, but with her large eyes and extraordinary night vision, Penny saw everything. Mr. Spider-Eyes was reclining against a large spiderweb. Franz Wolfbark was standing next to him, and they seemed to be drinking glasses of blood and eating bats on a skewer.

Mr. Spider-Eyes hissed sharply, "What are you doing here?"

"I got a note that you wanted to see me?" said Charles.

"*You?*" said Mr. Spider-Eyes. "You follow every rule to the letter every second of every day. Why in the world would I want to see *you*? I think someone is playing an April Fool's prank on you."

"Oh. Okay," said Charles, "I'll leave then."

"Wait," spoke Franz Wolfbark. "These two have seen us together. Surely we can't let them report what they've seen."

"Good point, Franz. Sorry, kids, looks like this is your unlucky day."

Mr. Spider-Eyes hopped off the web and suddenly turned into a giant spider. Franz Wolfbark removed his glasses and his tie, and turned into a giant were-wolf. Penny would have normally played possum right then, but instead, she was only thinking of saving Charles.

Penny tried to turn the door handle, but the door was locked.

"Please," Charles begged, "we won't say anything. Just make it a rule, and you know I'll follow it."

"Sorry," said Franz Wolfbark, "we can't take that risk and jeopardize our plan for the Ghoul Games."

Mr. Spider-Eyes and Wolfbark the werewolf lunged toward them. The kids were about to be torn to shreds, but at that moment, Penny felt something inside her that she hadn't felt in years.

Her voice.

It stirred in her belly then burst from her mouth as she screamed, *"Noooo!"*

And because she hadn't spoken in so many years, her voice had been building up inside her all that time, and it exploded with the force of ten fighter jets soaring into the sky.

It was so powerful that Mr. Spider-Eyes and Franz Wolfbark flew against the back wall like they had been hit by the wrecking ball from the goblin Halloween show. Seeing stars, they remained on the floor, muttering unintelligibly.

Penny saw a chain of keys sitting on the desk and grabbed them. She opened the door and pulled Charles out into the hallway. They ran as fast as they could back toward the lunch hall, but when Penny heard a loud roar from around the corner, she pulled Charles

into a crevice between lockers 217 and 218, a secret hiding place many of the kids used when they were in a pinch.

As they sat and caught their breath, Charles lifted his hand to fix his hair, but before he could even touch it, Penny was already fixing it for him.

When Penny finished, she smiled at Charles and Charles did something very strange by his standards. He put his hands in his hair and mussed it so that it was a complete mess. He then smirked at Penny as if to say, "*Fix that.*"

Penny laughed, and that made Charles laugh for the first time since he could remember.

"What happened in there?" Charles said through his laughter. "It was so dark, I couldn't see."

Penny, with her newfound voice, gleefully told him everything that had happened in Mr. Spider-Eyes's office, but Charles didn't hear a word Penny said because his ears were still ringing from her mighty yell.

20

Lindsey Learns a Lesson

Lindsey had long blond pigtails and was quite certain she was the prettiest girl at Scary School. Because she thought she was the prettiest, Lindsey also thought she must be the most popular, but the truth was, hardly anybody liked her because she seemed so sure she was better than everyone else.

Her only friends were Stephanie and Maria, who weren't very smart, so they believed Lindsey when she told them she was the most popular girl in the school. They thought being friends with Lindsey would make them popular, too. They weren't smart enough to realize it had the opposite effect.

Back on the first day of school, Lindsey, Stephanie, and Maria ran out to the hopscotch courts at recess. They were the first ones to get there and claimed Hopscotch Court #1 for themselves. It was the best hopscotch court because it was the only one in the shade. Lindsey took out a piece of pink chalk and wrote their names on the asphalt next to the court—LINDSEY, STEPHANIE, AND MARIA. Then, Lindsey shouted to the whole yard, "Listen, everyone! This is *my* hopscotch court because I got here first. I am the only one who is allowed to use it for the rest of the year. No one else can use it unless you have *my* permission. Got it?"

Stephanie and Maria crossed their arms and gave threatening looks to get the point across.

Lindsey

Everyone thought Lindsey must be some kind of tough Scary kid to make such a bold claim, and they all nodded their heads.

"I bet she's a harpy," Fred said to Jason.

"No way," said Jason, "she must be Medusa. Don't stare into her eyes or you'll turn into stone."

"Yeah, I bet that's it," said Johnny.

"Yeah, she's definitely Medusa," said Fred.

The rumor quickly spread that Lindsey was the young Medusa, and everyone on the playground turned around and dared not look at her.

"Well, that worked well," said Lindsey to Stephanie and Maria. "You see, when you're the most popular girl, you get that kind of respect."

"Um . . . no one's even looking at us," Maria grumbled.

"Of course," said Lindsey. "It's because we're so pretty. They don't want to be reminded of how ugly they are."

"Oh. Right."

The other thing Lindsey loved (besides hopscotch) was dancing. She took dance classes every day after school. She was very sad that Scary School never had any school dances for her to show off her moves. That's why she was so excited when Principal Headcrusher made this announcement on a Monday morning in early May:

"Students, as you all know, the Ghoul Games begin next week. I have just been informed by the gracious Mr. Wolfbark that students from the other Scary schools will be visiting us and attending classes with you all this week. The exchange will culminate with a school dance called the Dance of Doom this Friday night in Petrified Pavilion. I expect you all to be gracious hosts for our Scary guests this week and to make them feel at home. That is all."

Lindsey could hardly contain her excitement. When she heard about the dance, she screamed out, "Yes!" at the top of her lungs. A rush of thoughts were swirling through her head: I can't wait to go get a new dress, and new shoes, and a new haircut, oh, and I wonder who's going to ask me. . . . I bet everyone is going to ask me. . . . Who will I say yes to?

At that moment, three hideous monsters walked into the room—each one uglier than the next.

"Awoo-Aloo!" said the monsters.

"Awoo-Aloo!" said the class back to them, and the monsters did backflips.

"Hi, I'm Pob-Lob," said the first ugly monster.

"Hi, I'm Dorba," said the even uglier monster.

"Hi, I'm Gurk," said the ugliest one of them all.

"Welcome," said Ms. Fang. "I take it you're our exchange students from other Scary schools."

"Yop. We from Ogre Prep. We learn here. We need seat."

And so the monsters joined the class and seemed just as smart as any of the other kids, even though they talked funny.

"Sorry about the whole Golden Torch thing," whispered Jason to Pob-Lob. "I hope you weren't too mad at us."

"Huh?" said Pob-Lob. "Oh yesh! Thanks to you for stopping Golden Torch running! It saved many monsters from being smashed by trolls in contest to carry stupid torch. We were very gratefuls to you for that."

When class ended, Lindsey met Stephanie and Maria at their hopscotch court. They immediately began discussing all the details of the dance and who they were hoping to go with. Then the three monsters came up to the hopscotch court and looked right at Lindsey. It was the first time anyone besides Stephanie or Maria had looked at her in nine months, and she was a bit shocked.

"We play hop-hop with you humans," said Pob-Lob.

"Eww," said Lindsey. "In case you haven't noticed, we are the prettiest girls in school."

"You look just as ugly as every other human," said Gurk.

"Whatever," said Lindsey. "Maybe you can't tell,

but we are definitely the prettiest, and we do not play with ugly monsters like you, so go find some other weirdos to play 'hop-hop' with."

The three monsters *grrr*ed and walked away, then played a very nice game of hopscotch with Rachael and Raychel.

It was Thursday afternoon. The day before the Dance of Doom, and nobody had asked Lindsey to go to the dance yet. Everyone must be scared to ask me because I'm so pretty and they'll think I'll say no, she thought. I guess I'll have to ask someone myself.

She caught Fred in the hallway and said, "It's your lucky day, Fred. I want you to take me to the Dance of Doom."

"Sorry," said Fred. "I'm going with Rachael."

"Oh, are you sure you don't want to drop her for me?"

"Yes, I'm sure," said Fred, trying not to make eye contact.

Next, Lindsey asked Jason, but he was going with Frank (which is pronounced "Rachel"). Johnny was going with Petunia, Peter was going with Cindy Chan, and Ramon was going with Wendy Crumkin. Everyone had a date already!

During lunch, she thought to herself, I can't believe

I'm going to do this, and she went up to the skinny, geeky Charles Nukid and asked him to the dance.

"Sorry," said Charles. "I'm going with Penny Possum."

Friday at recess, Lindsey was playing hopscotch with Stephanie and Maria.

"I guess we'll all just have to go to the dance together," she said to them.

"Actually," said Stephanie, "I'm going with Benny Porter. He just came back as a zombie."

"Yeah, and I'm going with Antonio. He's a vampire in the sixth grade," said Maria.

"So you two have dates, and I don't?" said Lindsey, astonished.

"Yeah."

That made Lindsey snap, and she yelled out to the whole school yard, "Don't any of you realize how pretty I am?"

Then she burst into tears and ran out of the school yard. She curled up in a corner behind the lockers and continued crying.

Eventually someone came and found her. She looked up, expecting to see Stephanie or Maria, but instead she saw Gurk, the ugliest exchange-monster of them all. His face looked something like a rotten head of broccoli. He had squinty eyes, a pig's snout, and a forked tongue.

"What wrong, human girl?" Gurk asked.

"None of your business!" she snapped back.

"My name Gurk," he said. "You go to Dance of Doom with Gurk?"

Lindsey looked up at him and could only retch.

"Ugh!" she said. "You're the ugliest thing I've ever seen. I would rather go alone, thank you!"

"Okay," said Gurk. "Gurk understands. You do Gurk a favor though?"

"What?"

"Tell Gurk if his monster dance is good or not."

Lindsey chuckled and rolled her eyes. "Okay," she said. "This ought to be good."

Gurk put a music player on the ground and turned it on. A hit song blasted, and he started dancing.

Lindsey's jaw dropped. He was incredible. He was better than Justin Timberlake and Usher combined. She'd never seen anything like it.

"That's amazing. Are all monsters as good at dancing as you?" Lindsey asked.

"No," said Gurk. "Gurk just loves to dance. No one dance as good as Gurk."

"Well, you are fantastic," Lindsey said. Then she got up and started to show Gurk her own moves.

"Wow!" said Gurk. "You good dancer, too!"

"Thanks! We should totally go to the dance together."

Lindsey couldn't believe she'd said that. She just never wanted to stop dancing with Gurk.

"But you said no already," said Gurk.

"I was just kidding," she fibbed. "It's what humans do sometimes."

"Oh. Okay. Yaaay!"

That night, Gurk and Lindsey walked into Petrified Pavilion together for the Dance of Doom. She was wearing her new white dress and her new red shoes, and he was wearing a bright blue suit.

There were some snickers when they walked in and stepped onto the dance floor. No one could believe they had come together.

Then the music started. Lindsey and Gurk grasped hands and began dancing together. All the snickering ceased, and the whole crowd immediately formed a circle around them and watched Lindsey and Gurk do the most amazing dance anyone had ever seen. There were gasps, cheers, and shouts for more. No one could believe the spectacular display they were witnessing.

As the song was finishing, Gurk tossed Lindsey thirty feet in the air, spinning her like a top. Her dress spun so fast, it held her up in the air like a helicopter, and she flew around the pavilion to waves of applause and celebratory screams. Then she dove down to Gurk, and he caught her in a dramatic

finishing pose just as the song ended.

For the first time in her life, Lindsey actually *was* the most popular girl in school.

After the dance, Lindsey gave Gurk a kiss goodnight. Gurk's green face turned red, and Lindsey laughed.

She never judged anyone by their looks again.

Lindsey made more friends that last month of school than she ever had before.

21
Ghoul Games Week

A side from being the nicest teacher at Scary School, Ms. Fang is also a world-class checkers player. Last summer, she went back home to Transylvania to play in the Vampire Checkers Championship.

She made it all the way to the finals and was matched against five-time checkers champion Count Checkula for the grand prize. By the end, she was down to one piece left against his four kings. In an amazing maneuver, she performed a quadruple jump to win to the game. The problem was, she was moving at super-fast

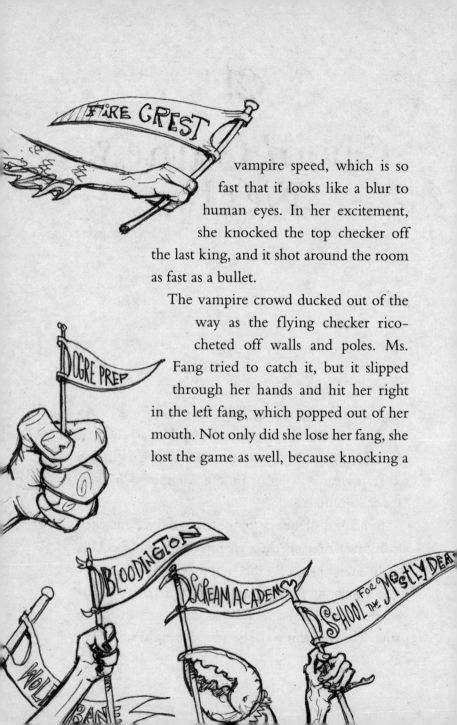

vampire speed, which is so fast that it looks like a blur to human eyes. In her excitement, she knocked the top checker off the last king, and it shot around the room as fast as a bullet.

The vampire crowd ducked out of the way as the flying checker ricocheted off walls and poles. Ms. Fang tried to catch it, but it slipped through her hands and hit her right in the left fang, which popped out of her mouth. Not only did she lose her fang, she lost the game as well, because knocking a checker off the board is an automatic disqualification in vampire checkers.

Ms. Fang was crushed. That's why she was in such a foul mood the first day of school.

However, she found redemption during the school year when the students in her checkers club went on to win the state championship, led by their captain, Wendy Crumkin. Now they faced the ultimate test in the Ghoul Games, as they would be matched against the number-one ranked checkers team in the world from Bloodington Elementary in Transylvania.

It was May 10, the first day of the Ghoul Games.

The week leading up to this day had been a resounding success by all counts. The students from all the different Scary schools were getting along, making new friends, and learning about the lives of all the different Scary kids from all over the world.

Petunia and Frank made friends with three zombie girls from the School for the Mostly-Dead. Rachael and Raychel found four more Rachels to

be friends with from four different schools—Scream Academy, Wolfsbane, Ogre Prep, and Bloodington Elementary.

Everyone was supposed to be practicing for their Ghoul Games events, but they ended up taking time off to participate in all the fun activities going on.

Johnny, Ramon, and Peter went bowling with the three giants they were going to play against in basketball. Lindsey taught pixies how to play hopscotch. Jason and Fred joined a pack of werewolves from Wolfsbane and learned how to howl at the moon.

Charles Nukid and Cindy Chan were joined in class by a group of young dragons from Firecrest. On Saturday afternoon, there was a big water balloon fight at Scary Park, and the young dragons let Cindy and Charles ride them so that they could drop water balloons from the air. Then, Frank N. Stein pulled up in a brand-new truck, and a whole family of freshly made monsters unloaded box after box of freshly made donuts for everyone at the park.

The night before the Ghoul Games, there was a giant slumber party inside Petrified Pavilion. All the kids were put into four-member teams with students from all the different schools. Each team was given a list of items to find on a great scavenger hunt all over the school grounds.

A team composed of Cindy Chan, Pob-Lob the monster, a Scottish dragon named Errrragonne, and a vampire named Sunny collected the first item on the list when they managed to snatch Dr. Dragonbreath's magical dragon glasses by singing him his favorite song, "Puff the Magic Dragon." Dr. Dragonbreath was crying so hard, he blew the magical glasses right off his nose and into the hands of Cindy Chan. Then the team jumped onto Errrragonne's back and flew away before Dr. Dragonbreath could catch them, which was all but impossible without his glasses.

In the end, however, the team that collected the most items was the team of Wendy Crumkin, Count Checkula Jr., Gurk, and a giant kid named Lenny. They were the only team able to bring back a particularly vicious Venus flytrap named Orf from Scary Garden.

While every other team got caught in the jaws of the Venus flytraps and had to be freed, Wendy was the only one who knew the secret of taming them, thanks to her hours of extracurricular reading. She told her team that all they needed to do was make the Venus flytrap laugh and it would be helpless. Luckily, Lenny was an aspiring comedian and he told Orf the Venus flytrap his very best joke. You can actually hear Lenny tell you the joke himself at ScarySchool.com, so I'm not going to spell it out for you here, because I wouldn't do it justice. It's all in the delivery.

When Orf started laughing, Gurk yanked him out of the ground and ran toward the pavilion. Count Checkula Jr. was tickling Orf's roots to make sure he wouldn't stop laughing and eat one of them.

When the scavenger hunt was over, all the students convened back inside Petrified Pavilion, and each member of the winning team was given a giant shining trophy in the shape of a hyena—the most fearsome scavenger in the animal kingdom.

As Wendy, Count Checkula Jr., Gurk, and Lenny held up their trophy, the hall was filled with a symphony of cheers, roars, grunts, groans, shrieks, howls, hoots, growls, and screeches the likes of which no one had ever heard.

Before everyone went to sleep, a student from each

school got to come up to the stage and tell the scariest story he or she or it knew.

It was the most fun week anyone ever had.

As the children slept peacefully that night at the end of the great slumber party, Mr. Wolfbark lurked in the hall of Petrified Pavilion, supervising in coordination with the other teachers.

For a moment, he considered howling at the top of his lungs, just for the joy of giving the children an awful fright right when they were feeling most secure, but then he thought better of it.

Let the human children have a last good night's sleep, Wolfbark thought to himself. For tomorrow, they shall all be dead.

22

Let the Ghoul Games Begin

The following day, the Ghoul Games commenced with a spectacular opening ceremony marked by a parade through the streets that ended at Scary School Field. As each contestant was introduced, cheers erupted from the massive crowd of supporters.

Three enormous dragons flew overhead and etched 651st ANNUAL GHOUL GAMES in fire writing across the blue sky. Hundreds of doves were released and quickly eaten by the hungry dragons and monsters in attendance.

Principal Headcrusher was introduced to the crowd, and she stood proudly atop the platform as her many monster friends from her days at Scream Academy cheered for their former arm-wrestling champion and good friend. Principal Headcrusher was on the verge of tears not only because of the gravity of the event, but also because she knew that if her students didn't win their chosen games, they could very well all be eaten alive and there would be no more Scary Shool by the end of the day.

Franz Dietrich Wolfbark pronounced the games open, and the first matches began.

Everyone ran to the frozen lake to watch Scary School play the abominable snowkids of Scream Academy in ice hockey. With Jason back at goalie, Scream Academy only managed to score one lucky goal. And with thirty seconds left, Fred scored a game-tying goal to even the score at 1–1. They played a scoreless overtime period, and the game ended in a 1–1 tie.

Since nobody lost, everyone got lollipops.

Mr. Wolfbark was seething and hissed at Principal Headcrusher, "Your kids got lucky thisss time, but you'll see! I've made sure they will *all* be eaten in the end."

Next, everyone ran to the basketball court for the big match between Johnny, Ramon, and Peter versus the three giants of Scream Academy.

As the game began, everyone quickly learned that height isn't everything in basketball. Johnny, Ramon, and Peter were much faster than the lumbering giants. Whenever the giants dribbled, the Scary School team stole the ball and got points off fast breaks. Soon the giants were so tired from trying to run them down, they could barely move. Ramon hit his three-pointers, Peter jumped over the giants for some monster dunks, and Johnny made all the great passes and racked up the assists.

The giants got their share of baskets, but in the end Johnny, Ramon, and Peter were victorious 77–71. Scary School erupted in cheers, and Mr. Wolfbark walked out to center court.

"Congratulations, Scary School," Mr. Wolfbark proclaimed. "Not a surprising result since the winners are Scary kids, are you not? You may claim your prize and eat these giants."

Johnny, Ramon, and Peter looked at one another, then said, "Um . . . that would be a big meal even for us. Can we just take the lollipops, please?"

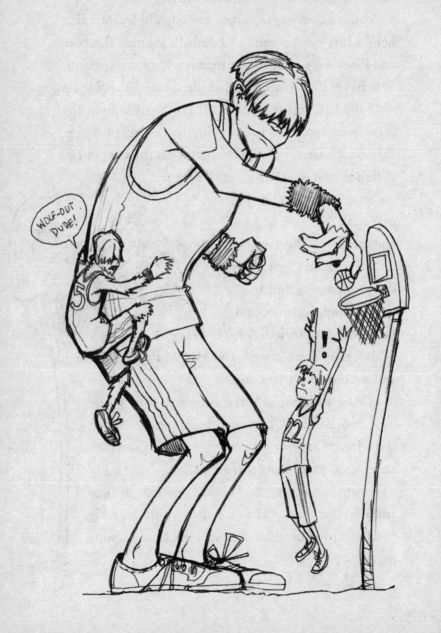

"Certainly," said Mr. Wolfbark, grinding his teeth. "That is your option, although the rest of you should not expect the same kindness from your opponents."

When they saw the giants sitting on the sideline very upset with themselves, Johnny, Ramon, and Peter walked over and broke their lollipops in half for all of them to share. It was the first time Johnny, Ramon, and Peter had eaten anything besides bugs for the last three months, and the lollipops tasted like heaven.

"I can't believe we ate all those bugs for nothing!" said Ramon.

"I didn't mind," said Peter. "I wish they made beetle-flavored lollipops."

Across the yard, Rachael and Raychel were playing their mind games against the Rachels from the other Scary schools.

Rachell, a twelve-year-old green-skinned witch from Witchbrook, finished the match with a dazzling mind-game display that went like this:

"Did you get a new haircut?" asked Rachell the witch.

"Yes," said Rachael. "Do you like it?"

"Sure," said Rachell. "I mean, as long as *you* like it."

"What does that mean?" asked Scary School Rachael.

The Scary School kids in the audience leaned forward on the edge of their seats, barely breathing as they took in each word.

"It's just, I would never wear my hair that way, but I'm sure it will work for you."

"So you hate it?"

"No . . . no . . . my opinion doesn't matter. If you like wearing *your* hair that way, then you should."

Rachael started crying, and the two Scary School Rachels were defeated.

Mr. Wolfbark smiled wide and proclaimed, "Excellent match, but Witchbrook is the winner. You may now eat your opponents."

Rachell looked at all the other Rachels and said, "Actually, there aren't enough nice Rachels in the world, and I would hate to deprive the world of any one of these very fine Rachels. I'll just take the lollipop."

Mr. Wolfbark seethed with anger. "Are you sure?" he asked, through gritted teeth.

"Yes," Rachell replied.

"So be it," said Mr. Wolfbark, handing her a giant lollipop.

And so began what many have called the Ghoul Games Miracle, when every single monster declined a delicious meal of human flesh after its victory because the monsters had forged such good friendships with the Scary School kids over the course of that week.

All the schools gathered inside Petrified Pavilion for the momentous Guitar Legend face-off between Charles Nukid and a young vampire named Ricky Rathbone. A sixty-foot screen was lowered, and Charles Nukid entered the stage with his Guitar Legend guitar hanging at his side. His hair was dyed hot pink and spiked into a mohawk, which Penny Possum had fashioned for him backstage. She had even smeared dark makeup around his eyes. He was dressed in the same school uniform he wore the first day of school—the gray shorts, white dress shirt, and polka-dot tie. All the girls screamed when they saw him in his uniform.

"What a rebel!" Maria shouted. "He's so brave *not* to wear the school uniform!"

As I'm sure you remember, *not* wearing the school uniform *is* the school uniform.

Charles patted the top of his mohawk to make sure every hair was perfectly in place, then signaled for the first song to start. It was a brand-new song by the Rotten Toads called "Smells Like Fly Guts." Charles had never heard the song before, but he was so skilled from his hours of practice, he got a near-perfect score on his first try. The whole pavilion was rocking, shaking, and bumping. Charles finished the song with an astounding knee slide across the stage. He leaped up and turned to the audience in triumph, his arm reaching for the heavens, his guitar vibrating with energy, his hot pink mohawk shining like a flag of eternal victory.

Seven girls fainted.

In the end, Charles narrowly lost to Ricky the vampire kid by just a few points, but instead of sucking his blood, Ricky decided to team up with Charles on co-op mode, and together they beat the all-time high score. The whole school went hysterical, and Charles was once again the school hero.

The monsters Pob-Lob, Dorba, and Gurk beat Lindsey, Stephanie, and Maria at hopscotch three games to two. Of course, Gurk wouldn't eat Lindsey because they were now best friends. Pob-Lob and Dorba were about to eat Stephanie and Maria, but Stephanie and Maria thought quick on their feet and used their skills in Monster Math. Stephanie and Maria both shouted out the smallest number they could think of.

"Negative fifty!" Stephanie and Maria exclaimed. Pob-Lob and Dorba became so frightened by such a small number, they scurried away with their spiked tails between their hairy legs and took the lollipops.

Mr. Wolfbark was so angry he was foaming at the mouth.

Petunia and Frank beat Mindy and Mandy the minotaurs in an exciting jump-rope contest, in which the minotaurs "jumped" out to a huge lead, but faltered when the rope got caught on Mindy's horns. By the time Mindy could untangle it, Frank (which is pronounced "Rachel") had reached ten thousand jumps first with the help of Petunia's precise counting. The minotaurs were aMAZEd. Ha-ha-ha. Sorry; I don't know if they were actually amazed, I just had to write that. I'm glad my sense of humor didn't die with me.

Next, Cindy Chan won an epic blame game when she managed to convince Marty the dragon that the Dark Ages were entirely his fault, even though they happened 1,500 years before he was born. Dr. Dragonbreath's history lessons had paid off tenfold!

Penny Possum lost a playing-dead contest to Zachary the zombie from the School for the Mostly-Dead when she took a tiny breath after lying motionless without breathing for more than fifteen minutes. Zachary won, having managed to actually die right there on the ground. Everyone was very impressed. Zachary would have eaten Penny Possum, but fortunately when he died his appetite died with him, so they left him a lollipop that he would never get to taste.

A very scary moment occurred when a team of terrible trolls from Cave Point took on the Scary School sixth graders in a wrestling match. The trolls won easily and were about to devour the whole sixth-grade wrestling team, when suddenly a loud *buuuuurp* was heard from the stands.

Everyone turned their heads and saw Dr. Dragonbreath heaving and belching and blowing bursts of fire from his seat in the crowd.

"Uh-oh. It's time!" Dr. Dragonbreath bellowed through another loud burp.

Dr. Dragonbreath stumbled out of his seat, crawled onto the mat, and all of a sudden, twenty-eight young dragons rolled out of his mouth in green balls of ooze and slime. He was regurgitating all of the kids he had eaten the first day of school—right in the middle of the wrestling mat! The young dragons stretched their wings and let out tiny roars and puffs of fire.

The trolls started kicking the young dragons out of the way to claim their delicious sixth-grader prizes, but the young dragons flew behind them and blew streams of fire

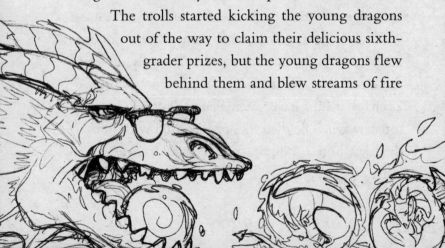

right onto their troll bottoms. Shorts aflame, the giant trolls were running around screaming "Waaaahhhh!" like babies.

"That's my boy!" shouted Randall's dad from the stands.

"Hey, Dad!" roared Randall. "Look at my awesome wings!"

"I know! You look soooo cool!"

The trolls ran out of the gym and jumped into Scary Fountain to extinguish the flames, crying, "Just give us the lollipoppies! We no like hot fire on bum-bums."

Mr. Wolfbark gnashed his teeth

and howled in frustration.

At last, the final event of the Ghoul Games took place: the checkers match between Ms. Fang's checkers club and Count Checkula's team from Bloodington Elementary. Scary School and Bloodington were tied for the lead in Ghoul Games points. The winner of the checkers event would win the Golden Elephant and the trip to Albania to meet the Monster King.

"This is where your luck runs out," said Mr. Wolfbark to Principal Headcrusher. "You've been fortunate your whole life just to have survived, but now you'll see what happens when humans match wits with a superior species."

The matches began, and the vampire kids from Bloodington took a commanding lead. Their hands moved so fast across the checkers board that Ms. Fang's team couldn't even follow their moves.

Scary School staged a late comeback in doubles play, and the two teams were even going into the final game, which would decide the winner. The match featured Scary School's best player, Wendy Crumkin, and Bloodington's best player, Count Checkula Jr., the ten-year-old son of Count Checkula.

It was a very tight match. As the checkers dwindled down, Wendy was barely ahead three kings to two. The tension mounted as Wendy took the lead two kings to one with time running down, but then Count Check-ula Jr. set a perfect trap and double-jumped Wendy for the win. Bloodington took the match.

The vampires leaped for joy and sang the school song:

Blood! Books! Blood!
Learning is so fun!
We love, love, love
Old Bloodington!

"Now," said Mr. Wolfbark, happily patting the young Count Checkula Jr. on the back, "I trust you shall drain these pathetic humans of their blood or I shall be gravely disappointed."

"Actually," said Count Checkula Jr., "I had a really great time with Wendy this week. We wouldn't have won the scavenger trophy without her, and she taught me how to play chess, which is a much better game than checkers, by the way."

All the vampires in the room gasped.

"So, I think I'd like to keep the Scary School team alive so that we can learn even more from each other. I'll take the lollipop. Blood-flavored, please."

Mr. Wolfbark was now quaking with fury. "The lollipop? The lollipop?" He couldn't contain himself

any longer and transformed into a fearsome giant werewolf.

"You leave me no choice," growled Wolfbark the werewolf. "If you won't claim your prize, then *I will!*"

Mr. Wolfbark lunged over the table with his sharp teeth glistening and his wide mouth agape to devour poor Wendy Crumkin. Wendy screamed, but just before Wolfbark could bite down, a giant hand grabbed him by the head.

"Excuse me," said Principal Headcrusher, "but I must protect my students."

She squeezed her mighty hand and crushed Wolfbark's head like a grape.

Everyone cheered.

Principal Headcrusher opened her hand, and everyone gagged at the gooey mess inside.

"Eww!" they all retched.

Then, Count Checkula Jr. stood up and made an announcement.

"Attention, everyone," the young vampire proclaimed. "I cannot accept this giant lollipop. The truth is, Mr. Spider-Eyes was spying on the Scary School checkers club and telling us their strategies. Mr. Wolfbark was forcing us to cheat, but now that he's dead, the truth can be known. Scary School deserves the Golden Elephant and the trip to Albania, as they would have certainly beaten us."

"It's true!" shouted Penny Possum. "Charles Nukid and I saw Mr. Spider-Eyes meeting in secret with Mr. Wolfbark!"

Everyone turned their attention to Mr. Spider-Eyes, who was slinking in the corner.

"How dare you betray your own school!" exclaimed Principal Headcrusher.

Principal Headcrusher tried to grab Mr. Spider-Eyes, but he made a break for the door. He flung it open, only to see his wife, Mrs. T, blocking his way out.

"Honey," said Mr. Spider-Eyes, "thank heavens you're here. We have to—"

Mrs. T didn't want to hear it, and she chomped down and swallowed Mr. Spider-Eyes in one gulp.

"Oh my! How could you eat your own husband?" the crowd asked, befuddled.

"I pity the fool who betrays his school," Mrs. T replied, licking her chops.

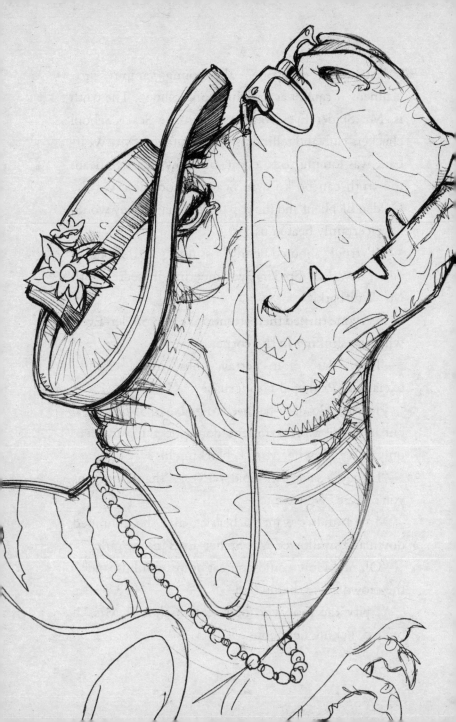

And so, Scary School was awarded the Golden Elephant, which was unveiled the last day of school and stands on top of a thirty-foot pedestal.

When Ms. Fang licked her prize lollipop, her missing fang magically grew back, so now her name is Ms. Fangs again. To my knowledge, that's the first time eating candy actually improved someone's teeth.

During the closing ceremonies that night, the students from each school were crying together as they said good-bye to their new friends. They promised to stay in touch and email as much as possible.

Once school resumes in September, the students will get to go on a trip to Albania to meet the Monster King and I can't wait to tell you all about it in the next book.

I *can* tell you that after that Ghoul Games, everything changed. Scary School is no longer considered a lesser school in the Scary community. Human children are now accepted into Scary schools all over the world, and humans and monsters are finally becoming friends for the first time ever.

So, whenever you're alone in the dark, or you're lost in a forest, or if you hear strange noises in the middle of the night . . .

You don't need to be as scared as you used to be.

Note from your author:
Derek the Ghost

Congratulations! You have survived your first year at Scary School.

You should consider yourself extremely lucky. I didn't think you stood a chance, but I guess even ghosts can be wrong.

However . . . you aren't finished quite yet.

Go to ScarySchool.com and take Ms. Fangs's Scary School quiz to unlock the *secret chapter* that will show you what happened on the last day of Scary School this year.

And here's a sneak peek!

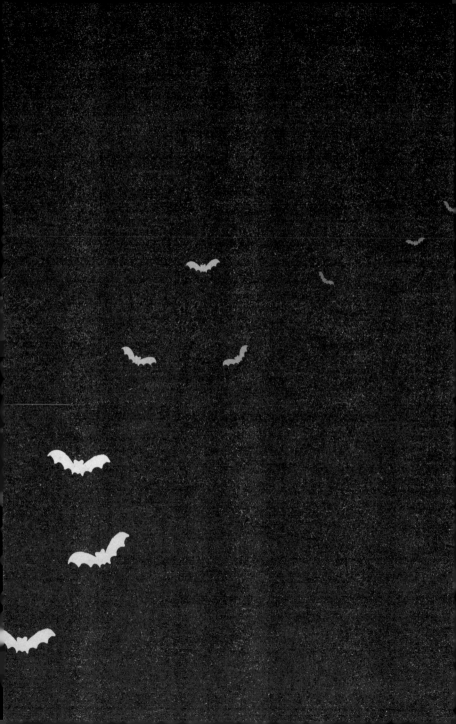

The Secret Chapter

It was June 11, the last day of school.

Principal Headcrusher announced to every class:

"As a special treat on the last day of school, Jacqueline has decided to let us all take a tour of the haunted house she has built in the school yard, which she just finished this very morning."

As you may recall, Jacqueline is my eight-year-old sister. She spent the entire school year building a haunted house for me so I'd have a place to live. Nobody believed that a haunted house built by an eight-year-old girl could be all that scary, but they were in for the biggest surprise of their lives.

To read the rest of this chapter, visit ScarySchool.com and take Ms. Fangs's Quiz!

The frighteningly hilarious adventures
of Charles Nukid and his scary friends
continue in

1

The Elephant Who Always Forgets

Petunia ducked frantically, barely avoiding being pulled into the Locker of Infinite Oblivion by the hideous ragged claw. It recoiled into the locker angrily, slamming the door shut.

I have got to pay closer attention, Petunia reminded herself, dusting the smudges off her purple dress.

She had gotten distracted searching the walkway for her friends.

Even though none of her classmates had contacted her over the summer, she had been desperately looking forward to school starting so she could see them. Petunia had not even heard from her best friend, Frank (pronounced "Rachel"), which she thought was very odd.

After the first few weeks of summer, Petunia had grown so lonely that she grew her purple hair back down to her purple shoulders. Her purple hair attracted honeybees, and she needed the company.

Petunia couldn't wait to find out who her new sixth-grade teacher would be. The teachers were always special. Last year, Petunia's teacher was Ms. Fangs, an 850-year-old vampire who was very, very nice. She only bit two kids the whole year.

As Petunia walked down the twisting main hallway of Scary School, most kids backed away from the bees circling her head.

Still not seeing her classmates, Petunia was very puzzled. Eventually she saw a boy she recognized. His name was Charles Nukid. He was from the other sixth-grade class. As always, his hair was molded into a perfect hair helmet on top of his egg-shaped head. He was wearing gray shorts, a white dress shirt, and a polka-dot tie, which was the official Scary School uniform that everybody else refused to wear because it looked so stupid.

"Hi, Charles," said Petunia. "Have you seen anyone from my class?"

"No, I was actually looking for Penny. Let me know if you find her. I have to hurry or else I'll only be on time for class instead of early. I'm always early. That's my own personal rule. Why risk it, you know?"

Charles had to catch his breath. It was as if he hadn't spoken to anyone all summer and had become overexcited when the chance came.

Petunia said good-bye to Charles and skipped toward her classroom. When she stepped into the room, she dropped her books in shock.

The room was empty.

Petunia double-checked her schedule. She was in the right place, Dungeon 5B, but there were no classmates and no teacher.

At 8:00 a.m., she peeked out into the hallway. It was as empty as her classroom.

Kids are *never* late for class at Scary School, because if a teacher is in a bad mood, well, let's just say there are a few lollygaggers who are walking around without all their toes or noses.

Petunia decided to take a seat and hoped that someone would come. She didn't dare wander the hallways without a hall pass. Even though the hallway monitor, Mr. Spider-Eyes, had been eaten by Mrs. T, the T. rex, during the Ghoul Games, the new hallway monitor might be even meaner. There was no point in taking the chance.

After a couple minutes, Petunia heard a loud thumping from the hallway.

Gathump. Gathump. Gathump. It got closer and closer, then stopped at the doorway. Petunia gulped.

Suddenly, the door burst open. In stomped something Petunia had never seen before. The creature had big, stumpy elephant feet, but the body of a man. He was wearing a tight-fitting suit and tie. His knitted brown jacket hung loosely around his humanlike arms. The creature had the head of a giant elephant, with floppy ears, long ivory tusks, and a trunk that

hung halfway down his body.

He looked at Petunia, then at a sheet of paper he was holding in his trunk.

"Hello," said the creature in a deep, goofy-sounding voice. "Are you the teacher?"

"No," Petunia answered, growing more confused by the second.

"Oh," said the creature. "Well, by process of elimination, I guess that means I'm the teacher."

Petunia stared at him blankly.

"What's your name?" the creature asked.

"Petunia."

"Petunia, eh? I'm going to write that down."

The creature placed the paper on the desk, then used his trunk to write Petunia's name on the sheet of paper. He didn't have much success as there was nothing holding the paper in place. It just kept sliding all over the desk.

The creature got frustrated. "This paper won't stay put for me to write down your name. Please excuse me if I forget it."

"Why don't you use your hands instead of your trunk?" Petunia suggested.

"Hands?" said the creature quizzically. He lifted his hands in front of his eyes and jumped back in fright. His hands were covered with fish scales.

"Oh my goodness! I have scaly hands! What kind of strange creature am I?"

"I have no idea," said Petunia.

"Well, thank you for pointing these out to me, young lady. I couldn't see them because my trunk was in the way. Tell me, what's your name?"

"Petunia."

"Petunia, eh? I'm going to write that down so I don't forget."

This time the creature used his hands to write down Petunia's name on the sheet of paper.

"Excellent!" he exclaimed. "Now we're getting somewhere. It says on this sheet of paper that my name is Morris Grump. Apparently, I'm the teacher for the sixth-grade class at Scary School. Hmm. I suppose that means you better call me Mr. Grump."

"Mr. Grump," asked Petunia, "do you know where the rest of the class is?"

"The rest of the class? No. Do you?"

"No."

"Oh. Well, we better wait here for them. I'd hate to go wandering around and get lost. I don't even think I'm supposed to be living on this continent. Don't elephants come from Africa?"

"Africa or southern Asia," Petunia replied.

"Say, you're smart! You're going to be useful!"

exclaimed Mr. Grump.

"Is that what you are? An elephant?" asked Petunia. "You don't seem to be a full elephant."

"Good point," said Mr. Grump. "I seem to be part scaly man also. I guess that means I'm the Elephant Man."

"But I thought elephants never forget."

"If you say so. The last thing I remember was trudging up a snowy mountain dragging a sack of coconuts behind me. The next thing I knew, I was walking down that hallway holding this sheet of paper."

"To be honest, you don't seem to know very much for a teacher."

"Well, I'm sure I must have done something *very* impressive to earn this position. I'll certainly give it my best. Now, what's the first thing you would like me to teach you?"

"Um. I don't know. Math?"

"Excellent choice! Math it is!" Then Mr. Grump's expression went blank and his trunk went limp. "What's math?" he asked.

Ugh, Petunia thought to herself. This is going to be a long year.

2

The Daring
Rescue

For the next hour, Petunia sat down with Mr.
Grump and taught him the basics of math.

Mr. Grump wrote everything down as fast
as he could, holding the paper with his hands and
scribbling with his agile trunk.

When first period ended, Mr. Grump was so happy
he couldn't wait for the next subject.

"What's next? What's next?" he asked excitedly,
jumping up and down, causing the whole room to
shake.

Petunia looked around the empty room. She was becoming very worried. There's no way the whole class would be gone the first day of school. Something must be wrong.

"We have to go find the rest of the class now," Petunia said to Mr. Grump.

"Okay," said Mr. Grump. "You lead the way."

"But I don't know where to look," said Petunia. "They could be anywhere."

"Hmmm," murmured Mr. Grump, scratching the top of his head with his trunk. "When I misplace something, which I do constantly, I always retrace my steps. Where's the last place you saw them?"

"The last place I saw them was at Jacqueline's haunted house on the last day of school. They all went into the Room of Fun, but I decided not to go in."

"Well then, that's the first place we'll look! Excellent remembering, um . . . um . . ." Mr. Grump slyly looked at his sheet of paper. "Petunia. I won't forget it again. Let's go, ummm . . ."

"Petunia," said Petunia, rolling her eyes.

Petunia led the way to the school yard. Jacqueline's haunted house stood beside the path that leads through the playground, which some kids like to call the slayground because of the high probability of injury or demise. Take, for instance, the alligators at the bottom of the slide. Brave kids still like to ride it, though. It's a fun slide until that last part with the chomping and dismemberment.

In case you don't remember, Jacqueline is my eight-year-old sister. She'll be nine in a month. She built the haunted house for me last year so that I would have a place to haunt. The school building was so uncomfortable. I don't know how living kids can stand sitting at those desks for so long.

Petunia and Mr. Grump stepped up to the front door of the haunted house and knocked. Neither realized that I had been watching them all morning and writing everything down. Naturally, I followed them to my haunted house, whereupon I made myself visible.

Petunia knew me and said hello. Mr. Grump had apparently never seen a ghost before and got very scared.

"Gh-gh-ghooosst!" he howled. He trumpeted a deafening noise through his trunk and started stampeding across the school yard.

In his panic, he ran into a tetherball pole with a *clang*, staggered about dizzily for a few seconds, then collapsed unconscious on the lawn.

"Don't worry. Your teacher should be fine," I said to Petunia. "Please come in."

I opened the door for her and we walked into the foyer. Ghosts circled the black chandelier above the great white fountain. Petunia remembered what to do. She plucked one purple hair from her head and placed it  carefully in the fountain's pool. Jets of water shot up and the ghosts cheered with joy. One flew down and opened the door to the rest of the house.

"Thank you," said Petunia.

"No, thank *you*," said the ghost, placing Petunia's hair on its white ghostly head.

As we walked down the haunted corridors, I told Petunia how lonesome I had been all summer with none of the kids around to write about. She said that she had had a very similar summer, with nothing to do but read.

"That's funny," I replied. "I couldn't read a book even if I wanted to. My hands go straight through them."

"How sad," Petunia said, trying to pat my shoulder, but whooshing right through me.

"Luckily, I have a ghost pad and a ghost pen that never runs out of ink, so I can write all I want."

We came to the end of the hallway to the door marked ROOM OF FUN.

"Is my class still in there?" Petunia asked me.

"I remember that everyone except you went in there on the last day of school. They started going down a slide and they haven't come out since."

Petunia opened the door to the Room of Fun, and a wave of sound crashed upon our ears. It sounded like a symphony of screaming and *whee*ing. Petunia bravely stepped into the pitch-black room and had to quickly catch her balance. She was standing on a ledge overlooking a deep, dark pit.

"Hello!" she called down into the pit. "Is anybody down there?"

"Petunia? Is that you?" It was the voice of her best friend, Frank, which is pronounced "Rachel."

"Yes, it's me!"

"Help us, Petunia! We've been going down this slide for three months and can't get off!"

Petunia thought it was very strange that they had been sliding downward for so long, but they were still able to hear her. At a normal rate of descent, they should have already gone straight into the Earth's core and been liquefied.

As Petunia's eyes became adjusted to the darkness, she began walking gingerly along the edge of the pit, feeling the stone wall with her hands. When she got to the other end of the room, she felt something strange. One of the blocks of stone was much warmer than the others. She knocked on the stone and it crumbled away like sand, revealing a glowing lever behind it.

As soon as Petunia pulled on the lever, the symphony of sound came to a halt. Petunia realized that the screams and *whee*s were not coming from her classmates. They were being blasted through speakers in order to mask another sound—the din of churning gears.

Lights came on, and Petunia could see into the pit. It didn't look that deep at all. Perhaps twenty feet to the bottom. Her classmates were piled on top of one another.

The walls inside the pit showed projections of a moving background so it looked and felt like they were sliding down, when in fact they were staying right in place the entire time! Just like a super-slippery treadmill.

Petunia began to recognize her classmates. There was Jason, still wearing his hockey mask. Fred, the boy without fear. The three Rachels, Wendy Crumkin, Penny Possum, Fritz, and even Ms. Fangs. They looked haggard and hungry, but were in a surprisingly good mood. Petunia guessed it was because they had been having nonstop fun for the last three months.

There were also empty water bottles and food wrappers all over the ground. Those items must have been regularly placed on the slide to keep the kids alive. My sister thought of everything.

As it dawned on the class what was really going on, most of them slapped their heads in frustration for not figuring it out sooner. Not even the teacher, Ms. Fangs, had had any clue.

The problem at the moment was that her class was still stuck at the bottom of the pit with no way to get out. Thinking quickly, Petunia sent her bees swarming down. The kids screamed, thinking they were being attacked, when in fact the bees were grabbing hold of them and airlifting them out of the pit one by one.

Soon the whole class was out of the pit. They were so grateful to Petunia that nobody made fun of her purple complexion for a whole week. Frank hugged her best friend so hard she could barely breathe.

Ms. Fangs was looking even more pale than usual.

She snatched a rat crawling along the floor and sucked out all its blood in one big gulp.

"Eeewww!" the class moaned, gawking at the disgusting display.

"Oh, it's not so bad," Ms. Fangs assured them. "Tastes like rat juice."

Wendy barfed.

As the class stepped outside into the bright sunlight, they noticed Mr. Grump lying on the ground, snoring through the side of his mouth. Petunia explained that he was their new sixth-grade teacher. The kids pulled him up off the ground. His tusks were stuck in the dirt, so it wasn't easy.

Mr. Grump opened his eyes.

"Are you okay, Mr. Grump?" Petunia asked.

"My head hurts, but I'm feeling better. Thank you, Petunia."

"Hey! You remembered my name!"

"I did, didn't I? My memory must be improving. Now if only I could remember why in the world I was dragging those coconuts up that snowy mountain!"

ENTER IF YOU DARE...

Will you survive

SCARY SCHOOL?

Read the first two books in the series to find out!